THE CHARING CROSS BOYS

Book Two

Sweet

Caroline

M. KATHERINE CLARK

Other Works by
M. Katherine Clark

The Greene and Shields Files
    Blood is Thicker Than Water
    Once Upon a Midnight Dreary
    Old Sins Cast Long Shadows
    Tales from the Heart, Novelettes
Love Among the Shamrocks Collection
    Under the Irish Sky
    Across the Irish Sea
    On the River Shannon
    The Land Across the Sea, an Emmet O'Quinn Short
Love Among the Shamrocks Collection the Next Generation
    In Dublin Fair City
    Song of Heart's Desire
    Chasing After Moonbeams
    You Don't Own Me – Coming Soon
Love Among the Shamrocks Universe
    Take My Breath Away
    Ghosted – Coming Soon
The Charing Cross Boys
    Set Fire to the Rain
    Sweet Caroline
    I Put a Spell on You
    Hold Me Closer
    You Don't Own Me
The Wolf's Bane Saga
    Wolf's Bane
    Lonely Moon
    Midnight Sky
    Star Crossed
    Moon Rise
    Moon Song, a Companion Guide
Dragon Fire
    Heart of Fire
    Will of Fire
    Born of Fire – Coming Soon
    Land of Fire, a Novella – Coming Soon
Sherlock Holmes Family
    Soundless Silence, a Sherlock Holmes Novel
    The Rest is Silence, an Edmond Holmes Novel
MacCulloch Castle Ghosts
    Silent Whispers, a Scottish Ghost Story
    Silent Night, a Scottish Christmas Ghost Story

For all my fans, thank you for your support of my boys! I am so excited to share not only Collins and Sweets, but Rhys and Kiter's from Set Fire to the Rain; Boyd and Vidar in I Put a Spell on You; Gareth, Dae-Hyun, and Lamont in Hold Me Closer; and finishing The Charing Cross Boys series Callum and Killian in You Don't Own Me! I love being able to write something you all enjoy!

Trigger Warnings:

There is some strong homophobic language from several characters at the beginning that the author condemns in the strongest terms, but it is written for the understanding of the character and hatred many if not all the LGBTQ2+ community experience daily.

Bullying makes a strong appearance in the beginning of the prologue. If this is a trigger for you, please skip to the break of page 5. This will skip over the on-page bullying.

Discussion of divorce and child custody surrounding wife's cheating.

Dubious-Consent for first kiss for which the character apologizes profusely.

If any of these are triggers for you, please proceed with caution. **Bullying and Homophobia are never okay. If you or a loved one has experienced bullying and would like to speak with someone, please visit stopbullying.gov/resources/get-help-now. If you would like to find ways of helping those who have experienced bullying, please visit StopBullying.gov.**

Prologue

It started just like all the other times. Sixteen-year-old Nigel Sweet hated this place. The older generation hated him because of the color of his skin, the younger generation hated him because of who he was attracted to. He would never understand why his father moved them from their home in the British Virgin Islands to the rainy, dreary, bigoted, London, England. His parents had always supported him, but they didn't understand him. How could they? His father intimidated everyone he met with his nearly six-and-a-half-foot frame and booming Islander accent. Nigel was a scrawny teen going through the clichéd teenage rebellion where black on black on black was all the rage. His black jeans, black T-shirt, and black hooded jumper along with the black and white converse, ratty black nail polish, and a black knit beanie on his head. The only splash of color was the tiny rainbow flag pin on his black backpack.

But that must have been enough. He ignored the racial and

sexual slurs from the four boys in the park as long as he could, but they didn't seem to appreciate it. He didn't want a fight. He just wanted to go home to his family, do his homework, and have dinner. He wasn't a threat to them. He didn't affect them in any way. They just wanted to pick a fight and he was the lucky one walking by.

He passed them as quickly as he could, but they followed. The smell of cigarettes and booze easy enough to smell. He wasn't going to get away from them easily. Hiking his backpack higher on his back, Nigel tried to hurry.

Two of the four walked around in front of him, the words coming out of their mouths made Nigel flinch. He had never been called those names and it boiled his blood. When the two stepped in his path, he tried sidestepping them, but they cut him off again. He paused and did not look up at them as he said softly, "please let me through."

"What? Sorry, can't understand you." They leered and tried to mimic his accent.

"I want to get home," he tried again.

"Oh yeah? You wanna know what I want? I want you, you little faggot, to leave and never come back."

"I am certainly trying to. So, if you'll step out of the way."

"You trying to be funny?" One of them gripped his backpack and ripped it off his shoulders.

"Stop!" He shouted as they tore off the rainbow pin.

"Faggot!" One of them shouted and threw it at his face. He blocked the pin with both hands flinching when it embedded itself into his palm.

"Got any other gay things in here?" They unzipped his bag

as one of the bigger boys tried to hold him back.

Turning the bag upside down, all Nigel's papers and books fell out including his favorite paperback of *Tuck Everlasting,* the one his grandmother had given him before she died.

"No please!"

"What's this?" One of the bullies grabbed the book and flipped through it. "Nene? Is that your lover?"

"No! Please!"

The bully flipped the book open to the middle and ripped it down the spine in two tossing the pieces into the mud. Nigel broke away from the one holding him and rushed to the book halves. Tears ran down his cheeks as he saw the slowly fading words on the front page as water bled the ink with his grandmother's final words to him.

Be true to yourself. Always.
Oceans of love, Nene

His whole body shook with anger as the bullies ripped up his tests, projects, essays, and threw his schoolbooks into the mud. Letting out a ferocious yell, Nigel raced to the main bully, the instigator, and tackled him into the mud. He straddled him and threw punch after punch, pummeling the boy's face into the mud. His hands hurt. His heart was broken, but his pain morphed into anger.

The other three grabbed him off the first bully and threw him into another mud pile near his book pieces. He curled into a fetal position holding the book to him as they kicked, spat, and jeered at him. The pain was intense. The hatred suffocated him. He felt hot liquid on his face and realized bully number one was pissing on him as the others kept kicking him and laughing at him.

"What do you think you're doing?" Another voice came from somewhere. "Leave him alone!"

"Gabe! Oh my God!" A female's voice screeched. "What have they done to him?"

"Call my dad, then get an ambulance," the male voice said. "I'm going after them."

"There now," the female's voice was soft and gentle, and he felt a soft fabric of a jumper wipe his face. "Easy, love. We're going to help you. What's your name?"

But he couldn't answer. He couldn't get a good breath. He heard her voice again, but he didn't think she was talking to him. Finally, the other man's voice came.

"Nance, how is he?"

"He's in and out. Those bastards peed on him, Gabe!" She sounded like she was crying.

"I got one of them. Subdued him at the woods. I know who they are. They're in fifth year."

"Why would they do this? It's awful.

"It is. Did you get ahold of my dad? And an ambulance?"

"I did. Your dad is on his way to the hospital and the ambulance is a few minutes out. I'll stay for the police. You go with him to the hospital."

"You sure?"

"Yes," she answered, and Nigel heard the soft sound of a kiss.

"Please," Nigel moaned. "Please."

"Hey, hey, mate," the man's voice was soft. "I'm Gabe. Gabe Collins. What's your name?"

He opened his eyes as much as he could and was greeted

4

by a man, a boy really, in his late teens, dark hair cut short, lazy but intense light green eyes, a kind, open face, and a soft smile.

"Nigel…" he said softly. "My name is Nigel Sweet."

"Nigel, it's all right. I've got you, mate." Gabe pressed a hand to Nigel's shoulder. "Try to stay awake, all right?"

But he couldn't and when he opened his eyes again, he was in the hospital with his parents huddled around him and his new friend standing in the doorway. When they locked eyes, Gabe smiled at him and Nigel felt his heart flutter.

Nigel could finally take a deep breath. The trial was over and he wouldn't need to be there for the sentencing. He took a shuddering breath as he turned his face up to the sky letting the sunshine fall warm on him. His eyes closed, he felt someone walk up to him and smiled when he caught the sweet piney scent of the boy he was falling for.

"In that light you might almost pass as cute, Sweets," Gabe teased and Nigel loved his nickname for him. No one else could call him that. Only Gabe. His Gabe. Well… not *his* in the way he wanted.

"And in those black slacks, you might not pass as gangly," he teased back.

"Hey, I'll have you know I'm the perfect weight for a wing."

Nigel chuckled. Gabe and his Rugby. "If I didn't know any better I'd say you were going to marry a ball. You love Rugby more than most people love their spouses."

Gabe barked a laugh and Nigel opened his eyes in time to

see his wide smile and the sparkle in his eyes. He loved that sparkle. He loved that smile. Gabe's wide carefree look darkened just a bit as he looked at him. Nigel knew what he saw. The scar over his eyebrow was still flaming red from where the bullies had hit him. Reaching forward, Nigel tried not to flinch or lean into his touch when his finger gently caressed the scar.

"You'll look hot with that. You know, most people love scars. I bet you'll get all the guys." Nigel tried to smile. Gabe had known he was gay from the first moment they met, hard to miss the pride flag pin imbedded in his palm. But he had never said anything about it.

Gabe's mother walked over to him and handed Gabe a gift bag as the family surrounded him. Gabe's parents, older brother and younger sister, and Nigel's parents and five-year-old twin sister and brother. Gabe turned back to him.

"So, ehm," he began. "I got you something." He thrust the gift bag in Nigel's direction with a blush staining his cheeks. "It's nothing major. I just saw it in the bookstore one day and thought you might... I don't know, it's stupid. Your parents had a picture of the dedication, and I was able to duplicate it. If you hate it, you can take it back or give it away."

Intrigued, Nigel pulled out the decorative tissue and stared into the bag seeing the familiar cover. He froze staring. His body wouldn't react apart from the tears suddenly swimming in his eyes. Slowly, reverently, he pulled out the paperback of *Tuck Everlasting.* The same cover as the one the bullies tore up. The gift bag hanging from his pinky finger, he opened the cover and his tears fell as a soft sob escaped him.

Be true to yourself. Always.

Oceans of Love, Nene

P.S. I can't tell you how awesome you are and how much I care about you.

You're the best friend I've ever had. You're like my brother, only cooler.

Friends forever,

Gabe

Nigel looked up at the man he loved and threw himself at him. Hugging him tightly, he knew it was all he would ever get. Gabe was straight, clearly, as his girlfriend giggled beside him, but in that moment, Nigel could dream.

Summer flew by and even with the vacation back home to the Virgin Islands with the Collins's, Nigel never hated August more than when it came around and Gabe stood in front of him in the airport heading home to pack for college.

"Look, I'm only a phone call away," he said. "France is dope. You should come."

"Yeah, maybe," Nigel replied rubbing the scar on his palm, a nervous tick he developed after the attack.

"Your dad said you'd be going back to London in a bit. It's only a couple hours by Chunnel. Promise you'll come to visit."

"I'll... do my best."

Gabe nodded and gouged the linoleum with the toe of his boot. "So... uh," he looked up at him through his lashes and Nigel's heart hammered. "I'll see you around?"

Nigel's heart crashed as he nodded quickly. "Definitely."

"Ready, Gabe?" his dad called, heading toward the gate.

"Yeah," he answered then looked back at Nigel. "Write? Call me?"

"All the above," Nigel promised.

"Cool," he tried to smile and then wrapped his arms around Nigel. Nigel sunk into the heat and scent of his best friend's body. "Always remember, Sweets, I'm here for you."

"Ditto," Nigel replied.

Gabe pulled back and Nigel mourned the connection. With a fond smile, a chuck under the chin, Gabe walked away leaving Nigel in BVI.

Gabe,

I miss you. I miss you so much. I wish you were here with me. I read under the palm tree again. Or at least tried to. All I kept seeing was you lying in the sun beside me, the palm shade playing with your cheek, the sun drying the droplets of sea water off your skin. The way your hair glistened in the light, so amazing, soft, and beautiful. I really miss you. Sometimes I feel like I can't breathe. Like those bullies are around me again. I know school is breaking for the holidays soon. But I haven't heard from you in a couple of months. I left London. We went back to BVI. I'm staying here for uni. They have a good program. I'm going to be a police officer. I figured it's the least I could do to give back after what happened to me.

You missed my eighteenth birthday. I missed you. I

wanted to tell you something. It's taken two years for me to gather the courage to write this letter to you. But Gabe, I love you. I've loved you since the first moment I saw you. I know you're not gay, but I had to tell you. I can't hold this in any longer. I needed to let it out. I needed you to know. I only want what's best for you. So please, don't feel obligated or whatever. Just tell me our relationship can survive this. I don't ask anything from you. I don't ask you to give me a chance, because you can't help who you're attracted to, and I know you don't like guys. But just put my mind and heart at ease and tell me you still care about me? I would never do anything to make you uncomfortable. I just had to tell you.

Please write back. I've enclosed my new address.

You are the best friend I've ever had. I guess it's only normal to have you be my first love.

Oceans of love,

Your Sweets

Months, then years passed by, and Nigel never heard from Gabe again. He knew he had truly lost the only man he'd ever love and his best friend. And it hurt.

London, why did I even come back? Nigel wondered as he walked through the rain to New Scotland Yard.

You know why, stupid, his subconscious said. *You hope to see* him *again.*

Pushing those thoughts out of his mind, he pulled the door open and shook out of his raincoat in the atrium rug so no one

9

could slip on the linoleum. Checking in, he headed up the stairs to the training room. After five years as a police officer in BVI, he decided he wanted to move on to a more daring career. He spoke to his commissioner, and he'd been put forth as a candidate for the Police Special Operations team and was offered the position as one of fifteen inductees.

"You must be Nigel Sweet," a thick Scottish accent said from behind him as he hung up his raincoat. Turning, he looked up to see who spoke to him. The man was tall with thick muscles but a kind and gentle face, the stripes on the shoulder of his uniform showed he was a higher rank.

"Yes, sir," he answered.

"Rhys Campbell," he introduced himself. "Second Commander. Call me Leo."

"Leo," he shook his hand. "Are you my commander, sir?"

Leo chuckled. "No, not yet, anyway," he winked. "I run the third battalion."

"Oh, I see."

"What brings you from BVI?" he asked as they made their way to seats near the front. "No offense, but I wouldn't give up sunny beach weather for this shite." He hooked his thumb over his shoulder indicating the window and the grey rain clouds beyond.

Nigel laughed and teased. "Yes, it's lovely, isn't it?" Leo let out a laugh. "No, sir, I spent some time in London when I was a boy and there's no chance of advancement in the small parish where I worked. And I was looking for something a little more... exciting."

"Well, we do exciting here but occasionally it's pretty boring. Glad to have you on the team."

"Glad to be here, sir."

"Campbell," another man called him. Leo looked back and nodded.

"Excuse me, boss man waits for no man." With a wink, he walked away, and Nigel decidedly did not look at his ass as he left the area. Nope. He looked away when he caught himself. *Dammit.*

More recruits walked in and soon the room was a cacophony of voices as the men and women milled about. Nigel kept to himself for a time unless someone came up to introduce themselves to him, then he was pleasant enough. He wanted to make friends. But he wasn't sure how. He'd never been particularly good at it. He was friends with people who decided they wanted to be friends with him. Like Gabe used to. Thinking of him invariably brought the heartache. He had never responded to his letter. He had never spoken to him again. With a sigh, he forced his thoughts away from the man but as if the universe was toying with him, he heard his laugh. Looking up, his brows furrowed.

There it was again.

His head swiveled around and there, by the tea trolly, like his mind conjured him, stood Gabriel Collins. The man Nigel loved. All color drained out of his face, his lips tingled, and his body went limp. Gabe was in the room. He was laughing at something someone said. His Gabe. Older, but those years looked damn good on him. His hair was still that dark silky color, his aquamarine eyes were still vibrant even if the skin around them crinkled more than before. His lips, those perfect pink lips were turned up into his signature dazzling grin. Before he knew what he was doing, Nigel stood and made his way over. His eyes glued to the man as if afraid if he looked away, he would be gone. He stood behind him, certain he looked like a stalker and hesitantly cleared his throat.

"Gabe?" he questioned.

The man who saved his life. The man he dreamt about for years. The one who had his teenage heart all aflutter, turned that blindingly beautiful smile to him. Confusion crossed his face, then surprise, and finally recognition.

"Sweets?" he questioned, and Nigel couldn't help his grin. He was back ten years ago lying on the sand, the sun beating down on him as he gazed at his best friend lying beside him, the waters of the Caribbean Sea washing over their feet keeping them cool. "Oh my God, Sweets!"

Setting down his coffee, Gabe grabbed him into his massive chest. Nigel went willingly and wrapped his arms around his back. He was home. Taking a deep inhale of Gabe's scent, so many memories from his teenage years flooded back to him.

Gabe pulled back too quickly for Nigel's taste but the smile that greeted him was perfect. "Is it really you?"

"Yeah," Nigel shrugged.

"What are you doing here?"

"I'm a new recruit. Spent some time back home in BVI as a police officer then transferred back to London."

"I looked for you when I came home from Uni, mate. I couldn't find you," Gabe said.

"Didn't you get my letter?"

"Letter?" Gabe questioned; his eyes genuinely confused.

Nigel's stomach pitched and twisted. "Oh shite, really? I explained everything." *And confessed my love for you.*

"I didn't get anything," he answered.

"You must think I'm a bastard just leaving like that with no goodbye?" *Just like I thought you were when you didn't respond to my confession.*

"No! Of course not! Mate, I'm sorry, there was a house fire while my parents were in Nice, and I guess maybe it got destroyed?"

"Oh, I'm sorry about the house."

"Yeah, lost a lot of stuff. But tell me what's happened with you? It's been ten years!" Gabe ran his left hand through his hair and Nigel's eyes landed on the shiny piece of metal wrapped around his ring finger. His heart lurched. His brain short circuited. He stared until Gabe lowered his hand.

"You're married." It was more a statement than a question. The evidence was hard to ignore.

"Yeah, I got a little boy, Hunter and another on the way," he bragged.

After a long moment, knowing he needed to say something, Nigel cleared his throat and forced, "congratulations!" The walls were closing in. He could hear the bullies taunting him. Feel the soft arms wrap around him. "I'm sure you and Nancy are very happy."

"Nancy? God no, mate that ended," he blew a raspberry "eons ago. No, Amelie and I met in France."

"Oh."

To lose him to Nancy, he was prepared for. She was sweet, kind, and gentle. She would have been a perfect wife. But to lose him to someone completely unknown was not something Nigel had been prepared for. Swallowing around the lump in his throat, he smiled, was properly apologetic for assuming, and properly happy for his happiness. When Gabe was called away by another member of the team and told Nigel they'd grab a beer at the pub that evening, Nigel took his chance and ran to the nearest toilet. Locking the door, he sat on the commode, wrapped his arm around his torso, and wept.

He would never have him. He knew that. Gabe Collins was straight. Never once looked at Sweet in any way that made him question his cast iron sexuality. But still. To have found him again after all this time, only to have the door firmly shut in his face, that hurt.

He hoped Gabe was happy. That was all he ever wanted for him.

Chapter One

Six Years Later

Gabe stared at his wife wrapped in the silk negligee he had bought for her for their last wedding anniversary. Her hair messed and a freshly forming hickey appearing on her neck, as the man moved around their bedroom gathering his clothes.

"How? How could you cheat on me?" Gabe breathed.

The man hurried to the door and left without a second glance. Amelie said nothing, only sat at her dressing table, reapplying her lipstick.

"Don't pretend this isn't your fault, Gabriel," she said. Her English was perfect when she wanted it to be but her French accent still colored the words.

"My fault?" He demanded.

"Oui, you're always gone with that team of yours doing god knows what."

"Saving England? The empire? The whole damn world!"

"Don't raise your voice to me," she said.

"You cheated on me with my sons in the next room!" He shouted. "Don't talk to me about raising my damn voice."

"And they are awake now thanks to you. They never woke while they were here."

"*They?* How many men were there?" He yelled.

She stood and walked over to him. "I told you not to yell at me."

"And you made vows before god to be faithful to me! You're my wife!"

Gabe felt her slap rather than saw it. His cheek stung. He honestly couldn't believe it. Breathing a laugh, he looked back at her. She had sauntered to the window and gazed out of the curtain. Gabe stared at her for a long moment taking in how he felt. His parents had been married over fifty years, his brother and sister-in-law had fifteen years under their belt, his baby sister was going on five years with her boyfriend. And he was in the middle with Amelie. They were eleven years in with an eleven and a six-year-old.

Commitment. Honor. Love. Those were the three foundations of a marriage, weren't they? That's what his father had said in his wedding speech. She didn't want the commitment. She didn't honor him. And love? That was a laugh. Their love had fizzled out a long time ago, if it ever actually existed. They were in lust, made a mistake, and he married her to give his child a name. Was he a horrible person for thinking his thoughts? He didn't care at that moment.

"Get your bags, I want you out of my house before I get

back."

She turned to look at him, the shock evident on her face. "And just where do you expect me to go?"

"I don't give a damn, Ami. Go to your mother's. Go to one of the dozens of men you shared our bed with. Just get out and expect divorce papers in the mail."

"Don't you dare put this on me," she said.

"I'm not the one who had the affairs, Amelie! You are. Do you honestly expect me to take you back? I want you out. Out of my life. Out of our boys' lives. You were never there anyway."

"Daddy?" His eldest son's voice came from behind him. He turned to see both his boys standing in the doorway.

"Heya, lads," he breathed.

"We heard shouting," his youngest said.

"Sorry, Colt. *Maman* is going to go stay with *grand-mère* for a short time, all right?" Gabe said.

"Are we going too?" Colton, his youngest, asked.

"No no, you're going to stay with me. Is that all right with you?"

The boys nodded emphatically. And apparently that was enough for Amelie to lose it. She launched herself at Gabe, scratching, kicking, biting even.

"Hunter, get a bag, grab some clothes and your school uniforms and get your brother out of here," Gabe ordered. "Wait for me by the car."

Amelie was insane, that was the only description. Shouting obscenities at him in French and English as she used her nails to scratch his face. The cut above his eye was particularly painful. Fending her off, he met his sons outside.

"What's wrong with *Maman*, daddy?" Colton whimpered.

"I don't know, Colt." He put the car in gear and pulled slowly out of the driveway.

"I didn't grab my football uniform for tomorrow's practice, daddy. I'm sorry," his eldest said.

"Hey buddy, tomorrow's a long way off. I'll come back and get your stuff," Gabe replied.

"Where are we going?" Colton asked.

Gabe stopped at the end of their neighborhood road and contemplated. Then, an idea came to him, "we're going to your godfather's."

Nigel had just turned off the lamp beside his reading chair. He had come home after the mission, debrief, and celebratory pub dinner and drinks with his team and collapsed into his favorite chair. Putting on some Dark Academia music on YouTube to calm his mind after being bait in the *Honeypot* con they pulled off, he read his favorite author's new fantasy gay romance book for over an hour.

The latest mission with his new team, The Charing Cross Boys, MI6's latest off-the-books assets was nerve wracking but easier than he expected. A group of them, five field operatives, one boss, and their team's admin created a tight group especially when everyone on the team was skilled, smart, and gay like him. Well, he chuckled to himself, not *everyone* on the team was gay. Gabe Collins, his police partner and best friend was straight, married, and a dad of two of the sweetest little boys to ever exist. But he was an Ally and treated like one of the boys even if he had never kissed a bloke before. Sweet would actively raise his hand as volunteer if ever Gabe wanted to change that particular fact.

Sighing, he took his wine glass to the counter and glanced at the clock. It was still technically early for him at 2200, but he was beat. He headed to the bathroom to wash his face and prepare his nightly routine when his doorbell sounded. His brows furrowed as he checked his phone still on silent from when he was reading. He had three missed texts from Gabe.

Gabe: You home?

Gabe: Sorry, I know this is random, but could the boys and I crash at your place tonight?

Gabe: I'll explain everything.

Hurrying to the front door, he opened it to see Gabe and his boys standing outside.

"Hey, sorry, my phone was off. Come on in. Hey boys!"

"Hi, Uncle Nige," the eldest said but his voice was quiet, almost sad.

"Did something happen? To the house? To Amelie?" He glanced up at Gabe and saw the claw marks on his face and a red angry mark on his cheek.

"*Maman* and Daddy are getting a divorce," Colton said.

Sweet's eyes widened. "What?"

"Come on boys, let's get inside," Gabe said. Colton rushed to Nigel and threw his arms around his waist, burying his face in Sweet's stomach. Nigel hugged him back and crouched down to be eye level with the little boy.

"I have some of those chocolate biscuits you like in the larder. Help yourself."

Colton sniffled but nodded and walked over to the kitchen as Hunter sat on the sofa and turned on the television.

"Bed in an hour, boys," Gabe called. Then, turning to Nigel he gave a tired smile. "Thanks for this."

"Of course, you're all always welcome here."

Nigel reached up to touch around Gabe's cut on his eyebrow. "Let's get that looked at. Come on."

A minute later, Gabe sat on the toilet seat while Nigel stood over him dabbing a cotton ball on the cut.

"I wasn't sure if you'd be... entertaining. Hence the texts," Gabe said.

Nigel chuckled. "Not on a school night," he winked. "I usually am my best company when I have a 0800 meeting in the morning."

"Good to know," Gabe replied then hissed as the alcohol stung.

"Sorry," he paused. "You going to tell me what happened?" Nigel asked continuing to clean the cut.

Gabe let out a sigh that broke Nigel's heart. "I found her cheating on me."

Nigel paused, blinked at him, then questioned, "are you serious?" *How could that bitch do that?* He wanted to shout.

"Yep, the boys were in their room asleep. I got home after our dinner and found her in our bed with another man. The bloke flipped when he saw me."

"Obviously," Nigel agreed. Not only did Gabe look like an MMA fighter, but he was also still wearing his tactical gear from earlier.

"Then she accused me of leaving her alone to fend for

herself or something like that. Then, when I raised my voice, which I know I shouldn't have-"

"Uh huh, don't do that. Don't blame yourself. You were angry."

"Yeah," he breathed. "But she slapped me. That's when I realized."

Nigel was pissed but he kept his feelings to himself as he placed the butterfly bandage over the cut. "Realized what?"

"That I didn't care." Gabe let out a pitiful moan and Nigel stepped back, giving him room. "I've been lying to myself and her for so long. I don't think I've ever... I know I loved her or at least I should have. She is the mother of my boys. But there's always been this... disconnect. Like with you, you always know what I'm thinking or how I'm feeling. You get me. She just... doesn't. I don't think she ever did."

Nigel refused to allow his words to affect him. He meant nothing by them. Pulling himself out of his thoughts, he focused on what Gabe was saying.

"...and then it was like this epiphany. We built our marriage on necessity, not love. But then I thought about my parents, and Frank and Sarah, and I realized, I'm a failure."

At the mention of his brother and sister, Gabe looked down. Nigel crouched low and cupped his face forcing him to look at him. "Don't do that to yourself. They have their relationships, you have yours. You cannot judge yours based on theirs. You don't know what their marriage is truly like. You see what they want you to see. Same with how you and Amelie presented your marriage to them. You are not a failure, Gabe," Nigel promised.

"No, I am. Something must be wrong with me if I can't

make my marriage work. I'm a failure as a man, a husband, and a father."

"Now, wait just one damn minute." Nigel stood in front of him again making him look up. "I will not allow that sort of talk. You are not at fault here."

"But I must be. She was looking for something I couldn't provide, so she looked elsewhere."

"No, she looked elsewhere because *she* wanted to look elsewhere," Nigel stated.

Gabe sighed harshly. "Tell me something, Nigel," he began. One of the few times Gabe called him by his first name versus *Sweets.* "I know you wouldn't lie to me."

"Never."

"Am I... unlovable? Emotionally unavailable? Do I smother people? Tell me, am I a horrible person?" Gabe's eyes pleaded with him, and the pain hidden behind them caused tears to pool in Nigel's eyes. He licked his lips and crouched again to be on the same level with him. He cupped Gabe's jaw and locked eyes with the man he had loved since he was sixteen.

"Gabriel Collins," he began. "You are the best man I have ever known. Your kindness, strength, beauty, personality, and love are second to none. You have so much to give and if she can't see that, she doesn't deserve you. You are an amazing man, friend, brother-in-arms, and father to those boys. There are so many people who love you. Me, included." His heart sped with his declaration. Gabe cracked a small smile.

"Thank you. I love you too," he said, and Nigel tried to keep his face neutral. Gabe had told him he loved him like a friend or a brother so many times, but it still stung even after all those years.

"Now," he lowered his hand and stood. "I've got some wine in the fridge, but it'll be too sweet for you. I have some gin and whiskey in the liquor cabinet. What can I get you?"

"A small whiskey maybe to help me sleep, but I've got to get the boys to school in the morning and we've got that meeting at 0800. Then, I have to swing by the house to get Hunter's uniform for his practice tomorrow."

"Do you want to go back there alone?"

"Not particularly." He motioned to his face and Nigel's hand clenched.

"She did that?"

"Yeah, but she was different. Like, it wasn't her, you know? She just flew at me."

"Talk to Kiter or Leo tomorrow and see what they think?" Nigel offered. "Leo" codename and alternate name for Rhys Campbell, was their boss on the force. Kiter, their current boss of The Charing Cross Boys, was Rhys' boyfriend.

"I don't want to bring them into it," Gabe said. "They have enough to worry about. And we're meeting the new recruit tomorrow. It's not the best time to talk about what the job has done to my family life. I'll talk to my dad and see what he says."

"Good idea," Nigel said. "Come on, I'm sure the boys are probably worried. The guest room has clean sheets."

"I'll sleep on the couch," Gabe offered.

"Not sure you remember how uncomfortable my couch is." Nigel offered his hand and helped Gabe stand.

"Hunter's probably already asleep on it. I can share the guest room with Colton."

"All right, if that works for you."

"It does for now. I'll have to figure out what to do next," Gabe said thrusting his fingers through his hair. "I told her to get out, but I seriously doubt she will."

"You know you can stay here, no matter what," Nigel said. "For however long you need."

Gabe's lips quirked into a half smile. He looked so tired. "Thanks, Sweets. I owe you one."

"Nothing is owed. That's what friends do."

With a gentle touch on Nigel's upper arm, Gabe left the bathroom and Nigel cleaned up the slightly bloody cotton balls, waste from the plaster, and the ointment he had put on the cut. He needed to calm his thoughts. Gabe had always looked out for him ever since he was a boy. He had been his partner on the police force and defended him against their own colleague Bethel who had picked a fight with Nigel and beaten him up a couple months ago.

Sweet never had a chance to return all those favors to Gabe, until then. But he couldn't very easily hurt Amelie, that wasn't how he worked, no matter how much he wanted to. But to see the pain in Gabe's eyes, Nigel knew he would do anything in his power to save his best friend and the love of his life.

Chapter Two

Something woke Gabe. He opened his eyes taking in the vaguely familiar surroundings. *Right, Sweets' place.* His cheek throbbed and his body ached. Then, he felt movement at his back. Turning over, he saw Hunter trying to slip into the bed next to his brother.

"Hunt?" He whispered so as to not wake Colton. His son looked over at him. "Are you all right?" He shook his head. Gabe turned over completely and looked at him. "What's wrong?"

"If you and *Maman* get a divorce, and something happens to you, what will happen to Colton and me? Will we have to stay with her? Could we stay with Uncle Nigel?" Hunter begged.

"Son, what are you talking about?

Hunter looked away. "You have a dangerous job, dad. You always say so, So what will happen to us if you get hurt?" He turned tear rimmed eyes to his father.

"Oh son, don't you ever worry about that. Your *Maman* would take care of you."

"I don't wanna stay with her," he said harshly. "She yells all the time and one time while you were away, she hit me."

Gabe sat straight up in bed. "She what?" Hunter looked away again. "Hunter, look at me. Tell me what happened."

"She told me not to tell you."

Gabe got up and walked around the bed to Hunter's side. He knelt before him and took his small hands in his. "Hunter, when an adult tells you to not tell me something, you tell them *okay* and come straight to me and tell me what they said."

"She said you'd be mad at me."

"I would never be mad unless you lie to me." He raised his son's chin gently. "Tell me what happened."

Then he did, and Gabe's anger spiked. His soon-to-be-ex-wife had slapped his son because he had asked for one more scoop of cheese on his soup. Hunter's little sob broke Gabe's heart and he grabbed his son to him and held him tightly. "I'm so sorry you went through that, Hunter. I'm so sorry I wasn't there for you."

"But when you're gone again, what will happen to us? I don't want her to hurt Colt."

Gabe's heart swelled. His little boy was growing into a wonderful man, and he could not be prouder. He wasn't worried about himself. He was worried about his baby brother.

"I promise you, she will not hurt either of you ever again. I'm going to talk to your grampa and see what he says. He'll know what to do." Hunter wiped his eyes and nodded. "Now, get some sleep." Gabe glanced at the clock. "We need to get up in a couple hours."

Gabe held Hunter's hand as he walked him around to his side of the bed and tucked him in kissing Hunter's forehead.

"Where are you going to sleep?" Hunter asked.

"I'll be on the couch," Gabe replied.

His little face scrunched up. "Uncle Nige is right. That sofa isn't comfy."

"It'll be fine for three hours," he chuckled. "Sleep."

Gabe watched as Hunter closed his eyes, holding his hand to his little chest. Stroking his son's hair, he waited until his breathing evened out and Gabe knew he was asleep. Then, he slipped out of the room, closing the door softly behind him. Walking to the living room, he turned when he heard Nigel's door open.

Nigel popped his head out. "You all right? I thought I heard voices."

"Sorry, didn't mean to wake you," Gabe whispered.

"No no, you didn't. I had to piss, so I was up." Nigel walked fully out of his room wearing a pair of baggy pajama pants with palm trees on them and nothing else. Gabe's eyes fell to his best friend's bare chest. He had seen him shirtless before, hell, he'd even seen him naked in the locker room showers, but recently whenever his buddy, his friend, a man he considered a brother, had exposed skin, Gabe's eyes wanted to linger. Even odder, he wanted to touch it. Rub his hand up and down Nigel's chest, feel the wiry hair growing there. The expanse and rich coloring of his skin was beautiful. Nigel always had been the most beautiful man Gabe had ever seen.

"Gabe, you're staring like I have something on my chest," Nigel said and touched his pecs quickly, looking down.

"What?" Gabe questioned, watching his best friend's hand slide down his abs. He wasn't defined but he was trim. More of a runner physique than a gym rat like Gabe.

Then, Nigel was there, moving in front of him, touching him... well, touching his arm.

"What's wrong? Are the boys all right?" And that soft question in that soft, accented voice, broke him. He felt all of Hunter's words like a punch in his gut. His breath left him on a gasp and his torso bent toward Nigel. Sweet's hands held his shoulders. "Gabe?" He questioned, his voice worried.

But Gabe couldn't. He couldn't answer. He couldn't do anything. Nigel grabbed him and pulled him to his chest. Gabe's head rested in the crook of Nigel's neck. Nigel's arms wrapped around him, holding him tightly. Gabe rested his hands on Nigel's back and buried his nose into Sweet's skin taking a deep inhale. He smelled like coconut and leather with a hint of musk from sleep.

"Talk to me, Gabe. I'm here."

And he knew it. He felt those words to the marrow of his bones. His best friend had always been there.

"She struck my child," he mumbled.

Nigel's body went rigid. "She what?"

Reluctantly, Gabe pulled back and looked at Nigel's beautiful dark violet eyes. "She slapped Hunter. He just told me."

He could feel the contained anger in Nigel's body, like a panther coiled and ready to pounce on its prey. "What are you going to do?"

"I am going to the meeting at work with you tomorrow morning after dropping the boys off at school. Then, I'm going to call Dad and see about getting a meeting with him. I'll have to take the afternoon so I can pick them up in time for practice. I have to get their uniforms from the house sometime tomorrow," he glanced at the clock and shrugged, "today, I guess."

"I still think you should talk to Leo or Kiter. I know you didn't ask for my opinion, but please know what I mean," Nigel said.

"I do," Gabe reached forward and cupped his face as if it was the thousandth time he had done it. Nigel froze. His eyes fluttered shut for a moment, then he cleared his throat, and stepped back.

"What do you need from me?" He asked. "For tonight, I mean. Can I get you anything?"

Gabe took a shuddering breath and shook his head. "I'm just gonna crash on the sofa for a couple hours. I'll be fine."

Nigel's eyes landed behind Gabe onto the sofa where Hunter had left the blankets and a pillow. He was silent for a long moment, just staring.

"I'll take the sofa," Nigel said. "You've been through enough today. Take my bed."

Gabe swallowed hard and shook his head. "That's not fair to you. We come in like a whirlwind and take over your flat."

"I don't care, you know that. You and those boys mean the world to me. Now, I won't hear another word about it. Go, get some rest."

"Come with me," the words were out of his mouth before he could stop them. Nigel stared at him. "What I mean is, you have a big bed. We're not strangers. Share with me. I wouldn't mind." *Was that weird? It sounded weird,* but oddly Gabe only felt nervous as he waited for Nigel's answer.

Nigel stared at Gabe. He hadn't heard him right. There was no way he had heard him right. But he had said something, no, not just *something*, he had asked to share a bed with him.

"Ehum," Nigel began. "No no, that's all right. Honestly, that might be a bit awkward for you. I don't... ehm... I don't want you to think I'd take advantage of the situation. You're already questioning as you said back in July, so I don't want to make you confused."

Gabe stared at him for a long time, then looked away. Hurt crossed his features but he nodded. "All right, I'll see you in the morning, then."

"Gabe," Sweets called him back. "I'm sorry. I just... can't."

Gabe nodded dejectedly. "It's okay, Sweets. Thanks for worrying about me."

Nigel said nothing until Gabe closed the door to the bedroom and he was alone. "I always worry about you."

Chapter Three

Nigel kept glancing at Gabe as they drove to HQ after dropping the boys off at school. He had a restless night on the sofa, he really needed to buy a new one. That might be, he decided, his weekend mission. Sommerset Kiter, their boss had promised that weekend would be free to welcome the new recruit and that meant Saturday evening at the new gay bar around the corner from Kiter's and Rhys's place. Nigel would never get used to calling Leo *Rhys*. But ever since he and Kiter got back together it was harder not to, as *Rhys* was what Kiter called him. He had always been *Leo* or *Boss* to Nigel. *Leo* being his codename from when he was in His Majesty's Special Reconnaissance Regiment team The Zodiacs and the name he introduced himself as when they first met.

Nigel turned to Gabe who was quiet driving them in and studied him for a short time. Gabe didn't look over. "Gabe, I-"

"Did you know ManU is playing against Tottenham Friday? Sounds like a good game," Gabe interrupted.

All right, Nigel thought. *Not ready to talk. Got it.* "I didn't, that sounds like you'll have a good time." Gabe was a season ticket holder for *Manchester United.*

"I won't be able to go. Not with no one to mind the boys."

"If it's a matter of minding them, I got them. You deserved to go and have some fun."

"No, I can't do that. I need to find a place for us. I doubt Amelie will leave my house without force. I should have somewhere we can stay by Friday. Move in."

He's hurt. He's trying to hurt you. Don't fall for it.

"But yeah, it would be nice. There was this cute blonde bird making eyes at me last time. Wonder if she'll be there."

Nigel took a deep breath. Gabe knew all his trigger points. And Nigel couldn't help the sting of hurt. They pulled into the garage and parked.

"Look, I know you're hurt because of the last night. Honestly, I don't want you to be. I didn't mean to reject you, or whatever. You are going through a lot, and I didn't want to add to it. I'm your friend. You're my best friend. I'm supposed to help ease your burden, not add to it. So please, if you want to go, go. But don't do it out of spite. I love you, Gabe, you must know that, and I love those boys but I'm not going to make things more confusing for you. If you need to go to the game to get your mind off things, if you want to have sex with that blonde woman in the bathroom to feel something, then do it. But don't act like I did something wrong, all right?"

Gabe sighed and thrusted his hand through his hair.

"You're right. I'm sorry. My head's just all over the place. I wanted to be with you because I was being selfish. It would have been a mistake. Not because I don't want something I've never thought I wanted, but because last night, I was low. I didn't want to be *that guy.* Divorced at thirty-five, two kids, single parent, shit. I'm sorry. Can we just forget it happened?

"If that's what you want," Nigel said.

Gabe forced a smile. "Thanks, Sweets, you're the best," he said and popped the door to get out of the car.

Nigel took a moment to gather his wits and stared at the back of the man he loved. Ever since joining The Charing Cross Boys, Nigel had wondered what might become of his and Gabe's relationship. On paper, all the members needed to declare they identified with LGBTQ+ community. Gabe chose to identify as questioning, but Nigel knew better than that. Gabe had never shown any proclivities and he certainly never showed interest in him.

Pushing those thoughts aside, he got out of the car and plastered a fake smile on his face. They would get through the little bump in the road. All would be all right. The topsy turvy world would settle again. They walked through the garage to the lifts on autopilot. Scanning his card after Gabe's, they entering the elevator car.

As soon as the doors closed, Nigel felt his world spin one-hundred-eighty degrees. He was staring at the brushed steel of the elevator doors one minute, then at the intense face of his best friend who whipped around and stood in front of him.

"To hell with playing nice," Gabe muttered.

"Gabe, wha-?"

But he didn't have a breath to finish the question. Instead, Gabe stole his breath. It took Nigel a good few seconds to figure out his best friend was in his space. His best friend's hands were tight on his hip and neck. His best friend groaned. His best friend was... kissing him?

"Finally," Gabe moaned against Nigel's lips.

Nigel stood there frozen. He felt the warm, bruising press of Gabe's lips on his, but it was off. It wasn't right. He had been dreaming about the moment Gabe would kiss him ever since he was sixteen, but it wasn't supposed to feel... wrong.

After a beat, Gabe pulled back slightly and rested his forehead against Nigel's, panting. Nigel blinked a few times, his lips ached from the sheer force of Gabe's kiss. His body was tingling, but not from arousal.

"What...? What's wrong?" Gabe asked.

Nigel closed his eyes for a short moment. "Nothing," he forced.

"Sweets?" Gabe asked pulling back all the way. The heat of his body leaving Nigel.

"Nothing. That was... unexpected. That's all."

When Gabe didn't say anything for a long while, Nigel opened his eyes. His best friend stared at him, lips and cheeks pink, but eyes dark.

"You... didn't..." Gabe tried.

Nigel took Gabe's hand from his hip and placed it at Gabe's side. "That was... different. But we're nearly there. Let's table this, huh?"

Gabe pulled back as if he had been slapped, then the apathetic look Nigel hated was back. "Yeah, sure, whatever."

Ugh, Nigel hated that word. "It's not that I-"

"No, no, it's fine. Not a big deal."

"Gabe-"

"Look, we're here," Gabe stepped to the door and tapped his fingers on his thigh waiting for it to open. Nigel said nothing and once the doors opened, he wasn't surprised when Gabe raced out of the lift and down the hall to their offices.

I don't think I've been more humiliated in my life, Gabe thought as he hurried down the hall, more like, hurried away from Nigel. He thought for a second, remembering all the stupid shit he had done in sixth form and at university. *No...* he thought again. He'd never been more mortified. He wasn't sure what he'd been thinking in the lift, but it sure as hell hadn't been with the head on his shoulders. Nigel just looked so good in that light tan sweater and black slacks. The sweater color set off his dark skin and fathomless eyes. His biceps and chest were well on display and don't get him started on his arse. Encased in the smooth material of his black slacks, it was begging to be touched, freed, ogled, squeezed.

What is wrong with you, Collins? He berated himself. *Sweets is your best friend and you're acting like he's a piece of meat. He doesn't deserve that. Get your head in the game.* What was he thinking? He wasn't, that was the problem. Maybe he should find somewhere else for he and the boys to stay. He could ask his boss. Kiter and Leo just moved into a large three-bedroom flat. They'd have room, but then the thought of hearing them going at it was too much of a dissuasion. Still, he couldn't stay with Sweets. *What if,* a stone settled in his stomach, *what if he wanted to have someone over? Oh god,* that thought made him sick.

"Collins!" He heard Rhys' Scottish accented voice call. He looked up to see the six-foot-three-inch Scotsman walk over to him. Leo, Rhys' codename, had been his and Sweet's boss in the Police Special Operations branch of Scotland Yard until the opportunity with the CCBoys came about. The man was one of his favorite bosses and a dear friend. "Sweet not with you?"

"What?" He nearly choked.

Rhys observed him. "You all right?"

"Fine!" Why did he sound like a prepubescent with the high pitch of his voice? He cleared his throat. "Fine. Yeah, thanks, Leo."

"Need to talk?" Rhys offered. *Damn the man and his observational skills.*

"Yes, but not now. We have the meeting," Gabe answered.

"Damn the meeting. Somm won't start without me. Come on."

They headed deeper into the offices and Rhys stopped at Kiter's door. He knocked and waited. When no answer came, he opened the door and walked in.

"Won't we get in trouble if we're not there on time?" Gabe asked.

"Don't worry. Of anyone, he'll take it out on me and that's fine with me." Rhys bit his lower lip and chuckled. Had Gabe not been so wrapped up in his own mind, he would have laughed. Rhys walked around his boyfriend's desk and plopped down in the chair. Indicating one of the ones opposite him, Rhys waited for

Gabe to sit. Once he did, Rhys said nothing. Gabe couldn't meet his gaze.

"That's some cut on your cheek your sporting," Rhys began and instinctively Gabe touched the butterfly bandage Sweet had placed there the night before. Had it just been the night before? It seemed to have been a decade ago. Rhys waited for his answer and the elusive feeling of comfort finally came back.

"Amelie and I are getting divorced." Rhys didn't react. *He knew.* "What did you know?" Gabe asked.

"Not much, but I suspected," Rhys said. "She was never there at your boys' games. She always made up some excuse for not coming with you to police charity events or parties. Call me cynical but that's the behavior of someone who doesn't want to be around you. So who does she want to be around? I made my conclusions. What happened?"

Gabe let out a long sigh. "I came home from our mission yesterday and she was in bed with another man."

Rhys gave a sympathetic nod, then looked away. "Been there, mate." He took a breath and looked back at him. "What happened?"

"He left, we... talked. Well, I talked, she just shrugged. Then when I told her I was taking the boys, she flew at me. Scratched at me and well, you can see the result."

"What can I do to help?"

"Nothing right now. I'm going to talk to my dad, see how to get started."

Rhys nodded slowly but his eyes were still watching him. "That doesn't explain the blush you were sporting when you walked in. Nor the red lips you had. Something else happened?"

"Damn you," Gabe muttered. Rhys just smirked. "I kissed Sweets in the elevator."

Rhys' smirk widened. "And? How was your first kiss with a guy?"

"Sucked and not in a good way. He didn't kiss me back."

"Interesting."

"No, not interesting, humiliating, mortifying."

"Did you ask him why?" Rhys asked.

"No, I just got the hell out of there."

"You should ask him."

"Why?" Gabe questioned.

"Because only he can tell you what he's thinking, Gabe."

"I thought... you know, he wanted me, too."

"Because you're so irresistible?" Rhys chuckled.

"No, because... well, I thought he was in love with me."

"You *thought* a gay man was in love with his straight best friend?" Rhys' tone was cynical.

Gabe shrugged. "Happens all the time in movies."

"And because of that you thought it was okay to kiss him without talking to him first. Not asking if it was okay to kiss him. You just... mauled his face. His straight best friend?"

"I'm not straight! All right? Jesus, I've wanted Sweet since the first moment I saw him. Yes, I was married. Yes, I've only been with women. Yes, I'm this guy who gives off this *can't touch me* shit, but I want him. I've been in love with him since god knows when. And his rejection hurts, mate, shit, it hurts so much."

"I understand that and thank you for trusting me with coming out. I'm here for you. But, Gabe, you also can't just go around kissing guys you haven't told. Nigel didn't know. He thought you were straight. Your wife just broke your heart. He's thinking about the mission. Probably still coming down from being the bait. I know you're going through a lot, but you might also want to consider what he's going through. Talk it out with him. Also... *ask* next time? No one likes getting mauled, aye?"

Gabe's stomach was in knots. He hadn't thought about that. Sweet deserved the very best he had to give, and he was acting no better than the bullies Nigel had to deal with his entire life. That was one thing he never wanted to be.

"God, what have I done?" He gasped.

"Nothing that can't be worked out, all right?" Rhys stood. "But now, come on, if we are any later Somm might blow a gasket."

They walked out of the office, Gabe's mind churning over everything Rhys had said. And when he entered the briefing room for the meeting, his eyes found Sweet. Nigel looked up at him, his face guarded then concerned. He didn't deserve that concern. Feeling the bile in his throat, Gabe turned and raced out of the room, to the toilets. Vomiting up his coffee and breakfast from that morning, he groaned.

The door opened but he couldn't concentrate. The water ran and then he felt a presence behind him. A cool towel was placed on the back of his neck.

"I'm sorry," Gabe said softly smelling Nigel's leather and coconut scent.

"Shh, shh, it's all right." Sweet's voice was gentle.

"No, it's not. I never wanted to hurt you. I never meant... I thought," he leaned against the stall and heaved a breath. He stared at Sweet who had crouched down across from him. "God, I thought you wanted it... me. I thought... I read the signs wrong, I guess. I'm sorry."

Nigel stared at him for a long moment, until he took Gabe's clammy hand in his perpetually cold ones. "You didn't read the signs wrong, Gabe. But I would never have acted on it. You made it clear in the past you were straight and I'm not one to mess with straight guys. That doesn't mean I didn't fantasize or fall in love with you. But you're vulnerable right now. You've had a horrible shock and you're technically still married. You and the boys need stability. You don't need me clogging up your thoughts and making you question."

Gabe stared into those violet eyes, eyes so otherworldly Gabe was sure Nigel was a nymph or something equally as fanciful. He was so beautiful, it hurt to look at him.

"I'm sorry."

"Water under the bridge. Now, let's get back in there and greet our new brother, all right?" Sweets offered his hand to him and helped him up. Pulling him into a hug, Sweet spoke again. "I love you, Gabe. I'm always here for you and the boys. Please always know that."

Gabe nodded into his shoulder. "I do. Thank you. And thank you for being here. I thought I had ruined our friendship."

"It'll take a lot more than a kiss to force me away, Gabe. Don't worry about that." Sweet patted him on the back and they headed out of the loo back to the briefing room.

Chapter Four

Sweet had to compartmentalize his entire life. It was a survival mechanism, so it didn't surprise him when he was able to separate business and what happened earlier with Gabe. But just because he was able to separate, didn't mean he could forget. He sat next to his best friend in the conference room listening to their boss, Sommerset Kiter and as much as he tried to focus on the words, his mind kept drifting to Gabe. He heard every breath, felt every tap of his fingers, saw every rocking of his chair.

His best friend had kissed him. *And there'd been tongue! Ugh.* It was everything he ever dreamt of, so why did it feel so shitty? He told Gabe his secret, that he loved him, and had seen the sheer terror in his eyes. Gabe may be questioning, but deep down he had some issues. Not with gay people, no, his friendship with everyone in the room proved that, but with the possibility of being gay himself. That was the main issue. But Nigel had to push all of that aside. They were there that day to greet the newest member of their team, and Nigel was excited to see who Callum and Kiter had picked.

"So where is this new guy, boss?" Boyd, the youngest of the group complained. "We've been here hours."

"It's not even nine, Boyd, you'll survive," Kiter answered.

"Grumble, grumble," Boyd teased.

He was the only one on the team who was a civilian before CCB snatched him up. The greatest thief of their generation, Kiter had claimed when they were introduced. Nigel wasn't even aware there was such a thing, but he'd hand it to the kid, he was good. Kid, *Jesus,* Nigel shook his head. The *man* was twenty-one, but he couldn't even grow peach fuzz, not that it would look good on his porcelain-fine features. He was beautiful. All of five-feet-eight and maybe weighed one-sixty-five on a good day of muscle training. It was funny seeing him train with Rhys and Gabe in the gym. Such a dichotomy. But he was strong, no matter the daintiness of his features. And for as much as he talked, he said nothing, so it was tough to get to know him.

Once, when they had all gone out to eat and Nigel had asked where he was from, which he thought was a typical question to ask a coworker. Boyd gave him this elaborate tale of how his father was an ambassador to India and he was born in New Delhi. How his mother and father had both died in an earthquake and he was sent to live with his reclusive uncle in the moors of England where he met so many wild and enchanting things. But he fell out of a tree into a secret garden and forgot who he was so when his father, not dead after all but disfigured, came to claim him, he didn't remember him and ran away. He fell into the wrong crowd in London and was forced to steal for food but ninety percent of everything he stole was forfeit to the leader of the gang. Only then did Nigel begin to realize he was pulling his leg. His tale was based on a number of books. Among them were *The Secret Garden, The Little Princess,* and *Oliver Twist.*

He had been so engrossed in the tale; he didn't realize everyone around him was laughing until Gabe whispered in his ear. "He's having you on."

Once he realized it, he felt his cheeks heat and he leaned back in the chair. "Very funny," he had said, and Boyd winked. Then Rhys grabbed something out of Boyd's pocket at his massive protest and handed it back to Nigel. The boy had stolen his watch right off his wrist during the tale. Apparently, it was enough of an initiation for him, and they all still laughed about it.

"Eager to welcome the new guy like you did me, Boyd?" Nigel called.

"Or are you curious if he's single?" Callum asked.

"A bit of both." Boyd had no shame. "It's been a minute since I had a good shag."

"A minute is probably right," Rhys said.

Boyd winked at him. "Don't worry, baby, you're still my favorite lay."

The room burst into laughter as Rhys' face went bright red with mortification. Rhys had been taken in by Boyd when they met at a pub nearly six months ago and Rhys had invited him back to his flat only for Boyd to shag him and steal from him. That had been an interesting story to hear.

Rhys' boyfriend and their commanding officer patted him on the back in mock comfort. Rhys gave them both the two-finger salute making the room cackle again.

"Let's not upset the Samurai, shall we?" Gabe teased and it lifted Nigel's heart to hear the light tone in his voice.

"Ooh," everyone sang.

"Tosser," Boyd coughed into his hand.

"Wanker," Gabe coughed back.

"Well, what a... civilized conversation to walk in on," Marjorie, the team's admin and acting *mother figure* said from the doorway. Boyd and Gabe looked away making an *oops* face.

"Thank you, Marge, you're right. That was not a good conversation, boys," Kiter said.

"Like you've never done that before too," she scolded, and Kiter flinched. "Anyway, he's here. Should I toss him into the firing squad now, or let you reload?"

"Show him in," Kiter replied, then scanned the room, eyes resting on Boyd. "Be nice. We don't want him running off." Boyd saluted lazily and the rest of the team nodded.

The door opened again after a couple minutes, and Marjorie walked in leading a man who Nigel had never met. He would have remembered *him.* "Damn," he breathed.

The man was a giant, dwarfing everyone in the room and that was difficult with Rhys and Gabe there. He had to be over six-and-a-half feet tall with solid muscle. His arms were the size of Nigel's thighs. He had dirty blonde hair and his light eyes popped giving him a godly sort of image. Nigel swallowed some drool and heard Gabe's frustrated grunt beside him.

"Thor?" Boyd asked. Thor was a good term for him. The man looked like the god of thunder.

The man's eyes lighted on the young man and he let out a

breath. His entire face softened, and his eyes went almost dewy. Nigel couldn't say he wasn't disappointed. The man was a beast, and he always had a thing for muscle men. But it looked like his eye had been caught by the siren in their midst, almost like Boyd had weaved some sort of spell over him.

"Everyone, meet Vidar Jørgensen, late of His Majesty's SRR and newest addition to our team. I know you'll welcome him properly. Vidar," Kiter had the man walk to the front to stand next to him, the man's eyes kept glancing to Boyd. Once he stood beside Kiter, Kiter slapped his back in a friendly hello. "Vidar has experience in weapons and bomb disposal. He also was the K9 partner for the division. He will make a valued addition to the team, and I know I am excited to have him here. Vi, meet The Charing Cross Boys."

"Hello," he said. The team gave the appropriate response. "I am grateful for this opportunity, and I hope we can work well together. I was born in Norway but have lived in England since I was twelve." *That explains the slight accent,* Nigel thought. "My father played for ManU."

"Wait, what?" Gabe questioned suddenly interested. "He wasn't Oskar Jørgensen, was he?"

"He is."

"Holy shit, seriously?" Gabe breathed.

"Are you gay?" Boyd asked, ever tactfully.

Vidar flinched and Kiter placed a hand on his shoulder. "Boyd, you know we don't ask how anyone identifies. Just because you're open with your sexuality, doesn't mean everyone is. He will tell you when and if he chooses. Now, I want to run a few sims for our new friend here before we go to lunch. And according to

Lester, we'll have a new assignment shortly."

"Lester's still around?" Vidar asked.

Kiter nodded. "Still our boss."

Vidar's light eyes clouded. "How do you know the big boss?" Nigel asked.

"I..." he glanced over at Kiter.

"Go ahead, the important one already knows," he winked at his boyfriend.

"I went with Kiter to the party for the team," Vidar revealed.

"You were the date?" Callum questioned. "Boss, you never told me."

"Didn't matter," Kiter shrugged.

"They were hot, making out on the dance floor," Boyd said. Rhys cleared his throat and looked pointedly at Boyd. "Oh don't give me that, baby. I know what you sound like when you come." Boyd waved him off.

For a brief second, the room was dead silent until Gabe let out a laugh beside Sweet that made him jump and then everyone let out the much-needed break of tension.

Nigel and Vidar locked eyes. The poor man looked terrified. "Welcome to the team," Nigel said.

Chapter Five

After Kiter had the team introduce themselves, they all headed to the firing range in the basement. Always competitive with his shooting skills, Gabe was impressed with Vidar. He was the only one on the team who could keep pace with him. But he still won, which was the boost to his ego he needed.

They decided to run through a simulation and Gabe supposed he shouldn't be surprised Vidar was exceptionally good. SRR was covert and the best of the best for a reason. No one really knew what those boys did.

After their run through, Kiter coached them on the good and what needed improvement. Gabe was glad for the escape out of his mind. Ever since the night before and especially that morning his head was all over the place and it was nice to be able to focus on a mission... simulated or otherwise.

"Leo," Kiter turned to his boyfriend. "You're still slow on

the final stretch. You need to pick up the pace."

Rhys was nodding. "I know. I'm sorry. It's raining and my knee is acting up."

Gabe watched Kiter's face morph to the concerned boyfriend before he schooled his features and nodded once. Then, his eyes fell on Gabe.

"Where's your head today, Reaper?" He asked.

Gabe's brow furrowed slowly as he searched Kiter's face with confusion. "Sorry, boss? Not sure I understand." He shifted in his seat. "My part of the sim went off without a hitch."

"Not checking in? Doing your own thing? That's not what we do here, Reaper."

His brows furrowed deeper. "What?"

Kiter clicked a couple buttons, and the video of their simulation came up. Everything looked good up to a point and then Gabe cringed.

"Reaper, come in," Kiter's voice came over the video. *"Reaper?"*

"About to breach door in three-"

"Negative, Reaper. Wait for-"

"Two-one."

"Reaper, that is not the plan," Callum's voice was next.

"It gets it done, doesn't it?" Gabe replied.

"Reaper."

And then the green light of *Mission Accomplished* lit. Gabe swallowed as Kiter paused the video and stared at him. That wasn't how he remembered it, but the video wasn't doctored.

"So, I'll ask again. Where was your head? Because this? This kamikaze, Lone Wolf act isn't going to cut it. CCB is a team not a solo act."

Gabe took a breath before speaking. "My head was up my arse, boss. I'm sorry. I never wanted to come across like that. I have had some... issues at home and that must have bled into my work life. It won't happen again."

"Collins," Kiter sighed. "You're damn good. But I would have hoped you would feel comfortable coming to me. If there's something I can do to help."

"No. Sorry. I'll be more conscious of it. I didn't mean to put the team in danger."

Kiter was silent for a moment, then, "all right." He turned to another on the team and Gabe's stomach flipped. Dangerous thoughts entered his mind. He wasn't man enough for his wife. He wasn't gay enough for Sweets. He wasn't a good enough father to protect his son from his wife's abuse, and now he wasn't good enough at his job. What the hell was it all for?

His thoughts ramped up and he wasn't sure he'd be able to stay seated. But at the last possible second, he felt Nigel's hand slip into his and squeeze. He turned to his best friend who gave him a soft smile.

"That's enough for now," Kiter said. "Vidar, it's tradition for the team to take our newest member out for lunch and end the day a little early so we can drink together. Drinks are on me, boys. Let's head out."

Cheering, everyone stood and gathered their coats. It was a chilly day and the forecast threatened rain, as Rhys had said.

"Gabe," he heard Kiter call and closed his eyes for a moment before turning to him. "Stay behind for a second."

Gabe nodded and locked eyes with Nigel. "Go on. I'll follow

you." Nigel said nothing but glanced furtively between Gabe and Kiter as he headed out.

Once everyone had left, Gabe headed down the steps of the small lecture hall they used for briefings and stood before the small stage where Kiter waited, leaning against the table, his arms and ankles crossed.

"Yes, boss?" He asked.

"What's going on with you?" Kiter stated the question.

"Like I said. I'm going through some things at home. It won't happen again."

"Bullshit," Kiter grunted. "Gabe, you're one of the most focused men I know. And the least selfish. For you to do this," he motioned to the computer with the paused video. "Is unheard of. Talk to me. Maybe I can help?"

Gabe adjusted his raincoat to his other arm and let out a resigned sigh. "My wife has been cheating on me. I found out yesterday after our mission ended. I took the boys and we crashed at Nigel's last night. I also found out she had slapped my son while I wasn't there. I am also struggling with my feelings for my best friend. I kissed him today and he didn't kiss me back. It's all been too much."

Kiter let out a breath through puffed cheeks. "Damn."

"Like I said. It's a lot."

"What are you going to do?"

"Right now, I'm going to drinks with the team and try to salvage the disastrous first impression I gave Vidar. Then, I'm going to talk to my dad."

Kiter nodded. "It's still early. If you need to head out early and take tomorrow off, let me know. But know I'm here for you, as is Rhys. We care about you."

The tension in his stomach eased slightly. "Thanks boss. It would be helpful to have some time off to deal with this."

"Take it. No harm done. I meant what I said. You are an incredible asset to this team. And we will need everyone at their best. We have a tough road ahead of us. Soon we'll be going after the Rentai Cartel and finding whoever killed our brothers, Hesler and Darius."

"Thank you and I'm with you. Still just struggling through the levels of anger."

"Past disbelief on to proving you're man enough, now?"

Gabe breathed a laugh. "About ten minutes ago."

Kiter chuckled. "Good, I knew something wasn't right. Just remember you have nothing to prove, Collins. Not to me, not to Sweet, and not to your wife. She on the other hand, has everything to prove to you. Just know we're here for you."

"Thank you. We're crashing with Sweets for the time being."

"Good, he's always looking out for you. But Gabe, don't hurt him. Don't give him false hope if there is none, all right?" Kiter warned. Gabe nodded and forced a quick smile. "Now go, I'll meet up with you guys shortly. Got to speak with Lester. Order me a beer. And if you could tell my boyfriend to stop loitering at the door and come on in." He winked. Gabe chuckled but headed up the steps to the door. When he opened it, Rhys was waiting nearby.

"Your man wants you," Gabe said.

"What else is new?" Rhys teased then slapped Gabe on the back. "You good?"

He nodded. "Thanks. If you ever see me pulling shit like that again, punch me."

"I can do that," Rhys patted him on the back and winked as he entered the lecture hall again.

Before the door was fully closed, Gabe moved down the hall toward the garage. He was glad to have the rest of the afternoon off so he could deal with the shitshow his soon-to-be-ex-wife had thrown his way. Taking out his phone while he rode the elevator down, he sent a text to his father, the semi-retired solicitor.

Gabe: Dad, do you have some time to talk today? In say three hours?

His dad's reply came as he stepped off the elevator.

Dad: I can manage that. What's this about, son? Everything all right?

Gabe: Could I pop on by? Don't want to text it.

Dad: Of course. You're worrying me a little, son. What's going on?

Gabe: I'm fine, the boys are fine. Just need your advice. It's about Amelie and it's a pretty big decision. I'll be there around 1500 after lunch with the team.

Dad: Your mum and I are here for you always.

Gabe: Thanks

"How did it go with Kiter?" Sweet's voice shook him from his thoughts. Looking up, he saw Sweet push off his car and saunter over. *Walk... walk over. He isn't sauntering,* Gabe corrected himself.

"Fine, just wanted to know what was going on."

"Did you tell him?" Gabe nodded. "Good. What did he say?"

Nigel asked.

"He gave me the rest of the day after drinks, of course and tomorrow off if I need it, to get things in order. I was just texting dad. I'm going to head up after lunch."

"Do you want me to pick up the boys?" He offered and Gabe was again struck with how much Sweets meant to him.

"Oh that would be amazing if you wouldn't mind. I'll head to the house and grab their uniforms for practice tonight and drop them at the school."

"Send me the info. I'll get them a snack and get them to practice."

"You... you are incredible."

Nigel looked away giving an embarrassed laugh. "Uhm... let's go meet the team. I don't want to let Boyd scare Vidar off on his first day."

Gabe agreed and unlocked his car. They both got in and before he started the car, he reached for Nigel's hand. He was always fascinated to see how his pale skin looked so sallow and ordinary against Nigel's smooth deep chocolate coloring.

"Does what I confessed bother you?" He asked.

"No, why would it?"

"Just tell me we're good?"

"We're good. I promise, Gabe."

Gabe took a deep breath and nodded. Then, taking his hand out of Nigel's, he placed it on the steering wheel and turned on the car. He flexed his hand and tried to ignore how empty it felt before putting the car in gear and heading to the local pub they had chosen for their lunch to welcome Vidar to the team.

Chapter Six

Gabe drove in silence to his boys' school. His thoughts were loud enough without hearing the mindless sounds of *Today's Top Hits.* Lunch with the team was good. Boyd was Boyd and Vidar loosened up a bit. Afterwards, he ran home to pick up a few things including the boys' uniforms. Fortunately, Amelie wasn't there, and he had left before she returned. He didn't want to see her or have a confrontation when he was feeling low. He sat in his car staring at the house he had bought over ten years ago in the hope of raising his children there. But no. He would sell it. It was paid off, thanks to a nest egg from his grandfather and would give them some breathing room.

Taking a deep breath, he let out all the pain she had caused. He needed to let her go. It was difficult with nearly eleven years of marriage. The pressures of society to not be a statistic of failed marriages. The pressure from his family to be as *perfect* as the rest of their children. Even though they never said anything, he could feel it. Everyone had their own opinions of his life and he wished they would shut up. They didn't live his life, he did. And it was beyond time he realized that and stopped giving other people power over him and his life. He was a man, a father, a police officer, a spy, he saved the world countless times. It was time he saved himself.

With a final look at the house, that looked and felt more like a prison than a home, he put his car in gear and pulled off the easement, heading to the boys' school.

"Good afternoon, Mr. Collins. It's wonderful to see you. How are you?" The school receptionist greeted him as he entered. She always blushed and sounded breathless when he arrived, he wasn't sure why.

"Ms. Charles, good to see you as well."

She beamed. "Should I call for the boys? It's a little early but I'm happy to."

"No, no need, I just wanted to drop off their football uniforms. They forgot them this morning," Gabe explained.

"Oh, certainly, we'll get these to them," she took the holdall he had packed for them.

"I was also hoping to speak with the headmaster, if he's available," Gabe said.

"Let me check, sir," she picked up the phone at her desk and pressed a button. There was a pause, then. "Mr. Collins to see you if you have a moment, sir." She listened, then nodded and hung up. Smiling at him, she spoke. "Go on back, he's waiting for you."

"Thank you." Gabe hurried back to the headmaster's office,

a well-appointed room with a lovely view of the courtyard and mahogany bookshelves lining the walls. Gabe knocked on the open door, seeing the much older man seated behind his desk looking at some papers. He glanced up and stood.

"Come in, Mr. Collins," he said in a smoky posh voice, gesturing to the chair opposite him. "What can I do for you?"

"I have some... unfortunate news to convey and I seek your assistance with the logistics," Gabe began.

"Of course whatever I can do to help." They both sat and the headmaster leaned back in his chair.

"Mrs. Collins and I are getting a divorce," he said it quickly, like ripping off a plaster.

The headmaster's brows rose. "Oh my, I'm very sorry to hear that."

"Thank you. I expect it to get messy and I would like your assurance of my sons' safety while at school."

"It is guaranteed," he promised.

"Thank you. I would also like to remove her from being able to pick the boys up," Gabe continued. "They have confided some... inappropriate behavior and they no longer wish to be alone with her."

"That is unfortunate, but I understand and will discretely inform the staff to be on the lookout."

"Thank you. Lastly, their godfather, Nigel Sweet will be taking a much more active role in their lives. Picking them up, dropping them off, that sort of thing. I would appreciate it if he were given the same welcoming treatment I have always received and come to expect from Bernard Academy."

"That is our way so long as he has your permission to be

on school grounds and engage with the students. We will have him sign a background check consent form and then have all we need."

"I, unfortunately, do expect my wife to raise a fuss, especially if she cannot get the boys. I will provide all legal paperwork as soon as I speak with my solicitor, to whom I am going directly."

"Legally, it would be best for the school's reputation if we had something on file, especially since you both are still their legal guardians." The headmaster passed him his business card with his email address.

"You should have something in your email later today from my solicitor and I will get a certified copy to you tomorrow," Gabe promised.

"That would be helpful, Mr. Collins, thank you. And you may rest assured your sons are safe here and Mr. Sweet will be given every courtesy. To help in this difficult time so readily without any familial tie is rare indeed. I have always enjoyed speaking with him. Such an interesting life."

"He is rare. A kindhearted man who's equal I have never found."

The headmaster's eyebrows rose. "High praise. Tell me, my nephew is homosexual, and I would dearly love to introduce them, is Mr. Sweet by chance seeing anyone?"

Gabe's stomach knotted and he stared at him. "Ehum…"

"Oh forgive me," the headmaster waved him off. "Unprofessional and impertinent. Please ignore me. I will ensure everything we spoke of is kept confidential but is given the utmost diligence." There was a knock on the door, and he called for the person to enter but Gabe's ears were ringing. The headmaster's words banged around in his head like the bells of Notre Dame, and he was Quasimodo, forced to listen with no escape.

Whether he liked it or not, Nigel was still available for men to date, kiss, sleep with, and there was nothing he could do about it. He may have admitted he loved him, but that meant little in the grand scheme. Nigel would date. He'd hookup. Bile filled his mouth, what if he brought a guy home?

"Mr. Collins?" He heard the headmaster call to him, and he looked up. "Are you all right?"

"Fine," he forced a little too quickly and only then noticed another person in the room. Colton's Maths teacher if his memory served him correctly. "My apologies." He stood and offered his hand to the headmaster. "Thank you, Headmaster for your assistance on this matter."

They shook hands as the headmaster replied. "My pleasure. I'll keep an eye on my email for the document."

"I'll have it sent as soon as possible." With that, he left the headmaster's office and distractedly made his way to his car.

Sitting in the driver's seat, he paused and took a breath. He needed to get to his parents' house but was far too distracted at the moment to do so safely. His phone buzzed and he grabbed it out of his back pocket.

Sweets: Just checking in. Wanted to make sure you were all right.

A smile instantly crossed his lips as he typed back.

Gabe: Am now. Needed that. Just finished at the boys' school. Heading to see my parents.

Sweets: Glad I could help *Beaming emoji* Drive safely.

Gabe: I will. Love you.

Gabe sent it before he could think and immediately cursed. He hadn't meant to say that.

Sweets: Not sure we're there, but thanks?

Gabe: Sorry, typed too fast.

Sweets: Ha! Yeah, right *Damn You Autocorrect Gif*

Chuckling, Gabe replied.

Gabe: Exactly. Anyway, I'm heading to my parent's. I stopped off at the boys' school and dropped off their uniforms. I also told them to expect you to pick them up. Can you still?

Sweets: Of course! I'll be by a little early so we can get a little snack before their practice. I'll keep you posted.

Gabe: Thank you!

Sweets: *Snape "Always" Gif*

Gabe chuckled. Nigel Sweet was a complete Potterhead. He even had a Hogwarts Gryffindor robe hanging in his closet and had visited the Wizarding World in Florida USA for his wand and to experience Hogwarts. He had roped Gabe and the boys into watching the movies over the Christmas holidays a year ago. Gabe admitted they were good, but as a father, he just kept wondering when the adults would take over and help Harry. His boys loved them, and they all planned a trip to Florida the next year.

He sent back a smiley faced emoji and the eye roll one, then clicked over to his photo app. He scrolled through the camera roll, smiling at his pictures with Sweets. At the boys' games, dinners out, dinners in, walks in the parks, with the boys, without the boys, the solo pictures he took when the sun was just perfect and Sweets had his head turned just so with his sunglasses on, and the selfies Gabe had taken of them together. He paused on one selfie of the two of them at one of the boys' games. Snow was on the ground and they were bundled up with scarves, hats, coats, and gloves. Gabe had his arm around his shoulders and their heads touched as they leaned into each other smiling. Gabe's finger hovered over Sweet's face. Then, snapping out of his thoughts racing around his head, he swiped out of that picture and began scouring his photos for a picture of he and Amelie. The longer it took to find one, the more frantic he became. He had nearly hundreds of pictures of he and Sweets and virtually none of he and his wife. It was glaring evidence of how out of touch both he and Amelie had become. He couldn't remember the last time she joined them at the games, or the last time they went out to dinner together, either as a couple or a family. She had quietly removed herself from every aspect of their lives and he didn't notice. When he did find a picture of them, he stared at her eyes. She visibly showed no sign of interest in him or where they were... hell, it had been over a year since they'd had sex.

Was it him? Did he push her away? Did she somehow know he was gay or bi or whatever he was? He thought back to the times they had sex. He never left her unsatisfied. He always made sure she enjoyed herself, but could she have faked it? When Hunter was conceived, on accident, had she only married him so she wouldn't have to take care of him? She was never a very loving mother, leaving the boys to his care when he got home from work and many times called up a minder while he was at work so she could leave them. Too many times he had come home to a teenager caring for his infant and toddler sons.

Gabe's head hurt and he was getting a headache behind his eyes. He slipped out of the photo app and switched to his texts. Sending two texts, one to Hunter and one to his dad.

Gabe: Hunt, your Uncle Nigel is going to pick you and your brother up from school today and take you to practice. I'm heading to talk to your grandpa. I'll be back as soon as I can. I love you.

Gabe: Hey dad, I'm on my way. See you in an hour.

He put his phone away and started the car, determined that his whole deal with Amelie would be over in less than a day.

Chapter Seven

It was approaching three o'clock when Nigel said goodbye to the rest of the team still at the pub and headed to his car. He had just remote started it when he heard Rhys' voice.

"Nigel, hold up."

He turned to his friend. "Hey boss... sorry," he smiled and shook his head. "Still can't shake that."

Rhys jogged over to him, coming to a stop just in front of him, a soft smile lifting his lips. "It's nice to hear occasionally even if it's not true anymore." He winked.

"What's up? Did you need something?"

"Where are you going?" Rhys asked with a knowing grin.

"Gabe is at his parent's house." He didn't know how much he could say. He remembered seeing Rhys and Gabe come into the briefing room together, but he wasn't sure if that meant Gabe had told him. "So, I offered to pick up the boys from school and get them to practice."

"Oh, you did, huh?"

Nigel eyed Rhys, confused by his playful tone. "Is there something I'm missing?"

Rhys shrugged. "I dinnae ken, is there?"

"Leo, it's been one hell of a day, could you just tell me what you want to tell me?"

"Gabe told me everything. About what happened with Amelie and the boys."

"Great, it's his story to tell. But why are you here?" Nigel asked.

"I was just wondering how things are going. You know... now that he's becoming more... open to the idea of being with a man?"

"He told you he kissed me," Nigel stated.

"Yes," Rhys nodded. "He did tell me that."

"And did he tell you I didn't kiss him back?"

"It did enter the conversation, yes."

"Is that what you want to talk about?"

"Do you?" Rhys asked.

"Oh for god's sake, Leo just ask me what you want to ask me. I need to pick up the boys."

"Tell me why, Nigel," Rhys said. "I know you. You've been pining after him for years and now when he finally is interested... you aren't?"

"It's not that," Nigel countered.

"Then what?"

"His pride is wounded. His wife cheated on him. He's

vulnerable. He's hurt. He wants to prove he is a man. That's not the right head space to be in when you're questioning your sexuality nor is it the right head space to be in to experiment and test it."

"Maybe, but it might be fun to see."

"And break my heart when he decides it's not for him? No, thanks."

Rhys winced. "True, I guess."

"I'm not going to be some experiment for the straight little white boy. That's not me."

"No, but you also don't close yourself off to your friends," Rhys stated.

"How am I closed off? I told him why. He accepted it. It's over. Just because you're playing house and happy family doesn't give you the right to meddle in other people's lives." He opened the door of the car and got in. He refused the feeling of guilt as he drove away, but it gnawed at him and he wound up sending Rhys a text as he parked at the boys' school.

Nigel: I'm sorry for my outburst and what I said, Leo. I'm frustrated with a lot. I shouldn't have taken it out on you.

Rhys' reply came as he stepped into the school.

Leo: No apology needed, Nigel. You have every right to feel the way you do. I shouldn't have pressed. I'm just happy for you.

A second text came in as he approached the headmaster's offices.

Leo: Oh, by the way, Scorpio got us a chance to talk with KY. Thought you might want in.

And just like that they were back. KY, Nigel assumed, was Kyetti the mark they had conned and arrested a couple days ago.

Nigel: Definitely in. When and where?

Leo: Tomorrow. Meet @ work @ 1100 Kiter and I have an appointment beforehand.

Nigel: I'll be there.

"Mr. Sweet, how wonderful to see you again." Nigel looked up from his phone to meet the eyes of Ms. Charles, the school receptionist.

He plastered a smile on his face and stepped up to her desk. "Afternoon, Ms. Charles. I believe Gabe Collins came by earlier and informed you I'd be picking up Colton and Hunter?"

"He did, indeed. I'll call for them, if you'll just sign here indicating you're picking the boys up."

"Of course," Nigel signed the paper.

"And he did ask us to put you down for long term pick up whenever needed. That's this form. It just gives us the permission to run a background check on you to ensure we're doing everything we can to keep the children safe. Everything is confidential."

"Happily," he filled out the form asking if he'd ever been arrested or convicted of a crime, filled in his NIN number and signed at the bottom.

"Thank you so much," she said and took the form. As Nigel waited, he made idle chitchat with the Headmaster who had popped out of his office.

"Ah, Mr. Sweet," the headmaster's smoky smooth voice said. The man was nearing seventy but was one of the most attractive older men Nigel had seen. His salt and pepper hair was still thick on his head, though he had the receding hairline on his forehead most men had. His sunken eyes were kind, and he had the bearing of an aristocratic knight. In fact, Nigel could almost picture him as one of the great knights of old, or a king in some Arthurian legend. His smile was lopsided to the left and his jaw was still pronounced even if he carried a little more weight around the middle.

"Headmaster," Nigel greeted and shook his hand in a firm grip.

"Wonderful to see you. Mr. Collins was singing your praises today. Saying how rare of a man you are and how blessed he is to have you as a friend."

"I am indeed blessed to have him and the boys in my life."

"Of course, of course," he answered. "I am afraid I may have offended him though."

"Oh? How so?"

"Well, I am unsure if he mentioned anything to you. But my question was only meant as an inquiry."

"I'm afraid I do not know what you're talking about, Headmaster. I haven't spoken with Gabe since he left to go to his meeting," Nigel said.

"Oh splendid. I suppose he didn't wish to embarrass me. I appreciate it."

"I doubt a man like you gets embarrassed easily, Headmaster," Nigel chuckled.

"It's been known to happen once or twice," he grinned. "No, I merely asked him if you were perhaps seeing anyone."

Nigel paused and stared at him. "I'm sorry?"

"Allow me to explain. My nephew just came out. He's twenty-five and we all support him, of course, the man is first rate. But he's too... shy for his own good. I wondered if you would be perhaps interested in meeting him. Such a wonderful man deserves his equal."

"Oh, Headmaster, I am humbled by your praise," Nigel tried to think of something that would get him out of it. "Perhaps, let me consider? If your nephew is as handsome as you, I would be hard pressed to refuse. But, you see, I... just started at this new company and well between working those hours and helping Gabe with the boys, it will be difficult to find time for myself let alone a date. Especially for someone deeply loved by his family such as your nephew. I would hate to cause him pain or question his resolve. If however my circumstances change, I know where you work," he winked. "And I would be honored to even reach out as a friend."

"Mr. Collins was right. You are a kindhearted man with no equal."

Nigel swallowed his emotions. Gabe had sung his praises? Why didn't he respond to the headmaster's request? "May I ask what Gabe's reaction was to your request?"

"Oh," he waved him off. "I didn't give him a chance, I'm afraid. I realized the unprofessionalism of my question and begged his indulgence. But he was... quiet. And I daresay a bit distracted?"

"Uncle Nigel!" Nigel had no time to think over what the headmaster had said as the boys came into the office and Colton ran to him, throwing his arms around Nigel's waist.

"Ready for a snack before practice boys?" Nigel asked.

"I want chicken nuggets," Colton said.

"What else is new?" Nigel grinned ruffling the six-year-old's hair.

"Mr. Collins and Mr. Collins," Ms. Charles said and held a holdall. "Your father dropped this off for you."

Hunter took the bag and thanked her. The headmaster bent to look Hunter and Colton in the eyes.

"Right, now, I expect you at full form for the game in a couple days. Practice hard. Remember what we say at Bernard?"

The three spoke at the same time. "Honor before commitment. Commitment before all else."

"That's right, lads," the headmaster shook both boys' hands. Colton giggled as he did. "Have a good time. And Mr. Sweet," he looked at Nigel. "Do think over what I said."

"I will. Perhaps bring him to one of the boys' games? I am making no promises, but I've been in his position before and he needs friends too."

"I will tell him. See you tomorrow, boys."

"Bye, Headmaster, bye, Ms. Charles."

With that, Nigel walked with the boys, asking how their day was. The headmaster's words not far from his mind, but his thoughts also drifted to his interrogation of Kyetti in the morning. He drove the boys to the closest fast-food place and sent Gabe a couple updates via text as they ate. He let the boys' love fill him as he prepared his mind for the diabolical task at hand the next morning. He would break Kyetti. He had to.

Chapter Eight

Waving goodbye to his parents as he walked to his car, Gabe pulled out his phone. He had felt it buzz in his pocket as he talked to his dad but didn't check it. Two texts from Nigel lit his screen.

Sweets: Boys are picked up and we're on our way for a snack then practice.

Sweets: He is so your son!

The last text accompanied a photo of Colton with two chips in his mouth like vampire fangs or walrus tusks, making a silly face. Gabe chuckled at the ridiculously cute picture. As he was about to reply, another text came through, that one was a selfie of the three of them. Gabe froze as he stared at the faces of his three guys. Colton, at six, beamed, eyes squinted, ketchup all over his mouth and chin looking happier than he had in a few days. Hunter smiled in the picture next to him and though the haunted look was still there, it was dim. Nigel... his beautiful face and dark violet eyes stole Gabe's thoughts. Christ, the man was stunning. Absently, his finger caressed Nigel's face.

A knock on his window startled him. Jumping, he looked over to see his father standing on the other side. Rolling the window down, he breathed out.

"Jesus dad, you gave me a fright."

"Sorry," his dad looked sheepish. "Everything all right? You've been staring at your phone for a few minutes."

I have? "Yeah, fine. Nigel was just texting me. He sent this," he showed the picture of Colton with the chips in his mouth.

Gabe's dad chuckled. Then swiped to see the second one. The selfie. He paused and Gabe's stomach twisted.

"That lad really loves the boys, doesn't he?"

"Sweets?" Gabe questioned. "Yeah, he's a godsend the last couple days. He let us stay at his flat without question."

His dad was nodding sagely. "He's a good man."

"Yeah, he is."

"Good people are hard to find. Trust me, lad, I'm a solicitor. I've seen the worst, but one thing about that man even as a young man, he had this sort of innocence like the world hadn't touched him yet and brought him down. Now, as a man it's clear the world has hurt him. He's a gay black man, of course the world is not kind to anyone or anything they deem different. But he has turned that agony into something beautiful." Gabe's heart lurched. He wanted to protect Nigel from every evil that was hurled at him. Every unkind look, gesture, word spoken, anything that would wipe that smile off his face, Gabe wanted to destroy.

"Son," his father continued on a sigh. "You know your

mother and I love you no matter what, right?"

Gabe's stomach twisted. "Of course, dad." He tried to be light.

"And you can tell us anything."

Gabe swallowed the bile filling his mouth. "As proven by today's meeting, I think."

His father was quiet for a long moment, then nodded, patted the window frame, and smiled slightly. "I'll have the papers served to her today and file the custody request. Drive safely." His dad stepped back and headed up to the porch where Gabe's mother stood wrapped in her shawl.

Quickly sending a reply to Nigel, he pulled out of his parents' drive and headed down the street.

Gabe: Thank you for getting the boys. I'm leaving my parents now.

His phone dinged as he stopped at a traffic signal.

Sweets: How did it go?

Sweets: We're at practice. Boys are doing great!

Gabe: Went well, not sure I'll make practice. I'll pick up some dinner, if it's all right we stay with you again?

Sweets: Of course it's all right!

He smiled at the text then nearly dropped his phone when another car behind him honked. The light was green. Giving a courtesy wave behind him, he drove through the intersection.

The drive home was quiet as his father's words echoed in his ears. Did his dad want to tell him he knew about his feelings for Sweets? Was it a warning to stay away? Did he think Gabe would hurt him? His parents had been protective of Nigel ever since his father had taken the assault case against the bullies who hurt him. His father had to know he would never hurt Nigel. Not intentionally at least.

Pulling out of his thoughts long enough to figure out what he wanted for dinner, Gabe pulled into the market car park. He wanted to make dinner for Nigel and the boys as a thank you. Grabbing a shopping trolley, he walked to the fresh fish and meat. Eyes landing on a beautiful salmon, he finally decided what he was going to make and grabbed a bottle of wine for good measure as he headed to check out.

The flat was empty when he got there, fortunately Sweets had given him a key years ago and he let himself in. Placing the groceries on the counter, he went to the spare room to put the holdall he had picked up from home and unpacked a white t-shirt and grey joggers. He stripped out of his work clothes and changed. Syncing his phone to Sweet's Bluetooth speakers, he put on some music and got to work prepping the fish, roasting asparagus, and red potatoes.

It was about twenty minutes later when the door opened and he heard, "Honey, we're home!" in that playful islander accented voice. He grinned and turned from the pan simmering some seasoned rice to see his boys run in, dirty and sweaty, but laughing and smiling.

"Daddy!" Colton ran right to him and threw his arms around Gabe's hips.

"Hey buddy!" Gabe hugged him back. "How was practice?" He looked up at Hunter.

"It was good," Hunter replied. "I think we're ready to take on Barton Academy on Saturday."

"Great!" He loved the happiness in Hunter's eyes.

"Dinner's in ten, wash up."

"Okay, daddy!" Colton raced to the bathroom, Hunter right behind him as Nigel sauntered over.

"Hey."

"Hey," Gabe breathed.

"Something smells amazing."

"Good."

"When you offered to get dinner," Nigel began. "I was skeptical. I expected more burger in a bag."

"Not always," Gabe grinned. "It might surprise you to know, Mr. Sweet, but I am actually a good cook." They stared at each other for a long moment and Gabe would have given anything to know what Nigel was thinking. Then, after a long moment, Nigel broke eye contact and turned away. Gabe felt the connection end like a punch in the gut.

"What can I do to help?" Nigel asked.

"Uh uh, nothing, this is my treat. Thank you for letting us stay."

"You don't have to thank me, Gabe. You're always welcome. You and the boys."

"Still."

"Well, I'll never say no to dinner cooked and served to me by a man in grey joggers."

Gabe laughed one harsh sound then shook his head. As Nigel stood beside him, Gabe gently hip checked him and motioned with his head.

"Didn't I say to wash up for dinner?" His voice pitched low, and he grinned when Nigel shivered.

"Yes, daddy," he whispered and walked away, leaving

Gabe in a state he wouldn't want anyone, let alone his sons, to see.

After dropping the boys off at school, Gabe and Nigel drove to HQ. They had talked the evening before about the text Rhys had sent Nigel about interrogating Kyetti, the war criminal.

"And you're sure you're okay with interviewing him?" Gabe asked.

Nigel nodded. "I'm positive. I'm his type." He shrugged and watched as Gabe's hand tightened on the steering wheel. He slipped his hand over Gabe's tight forearm. "I'll be fine. I promise."

Gabe nodded. "Sorry, I just hate the idea."

They pulled out their security passes to badge into the underground parking facility. "I'm not overly excited either, but I won't deny it's exciting."

Gabe chuckled. "You always did like to get answers out of our suspects."

"It's acting and like a puzzle."

"It is. And you're a very good actor." He pulled the car into his spot and turned off the engine. Unhooking his seat belt, he turned to Nigel stopping him from getting out of the car. "Just promise me, you'll be safe."

Nigel let the gooey feeling of Gabe's concern simmer in his belly. He smiled softly and cupped Gabe's cheek. Locking eyes with him, he emphasized his words with a moment of silence before he spoke. "I promise, Gabe. All I'm going to be doing is asking questions. Leo and probably Kiter will be there with me the whole time. Thank you for your concern. But don't worry, okay?"

"Can I kiss you?" Gabe's voice cracked and with it Nigel's resolve.

Taking a deep breath, letting go of all the fear of the unknown and worry of future pain, he made his decision. "Yes, Gabe. You may kiss me."

Part of him thought Gabe would lunge forward and grab him, but instead, Nigel watched as his eyes grew wide with surprise, then closed for a moment, the look on his face one of ecstasy. When Gabe opened his eyes again, he slowly leaned forward and cupped Nigel's face.

Almost like a movie, one of those romcoms Nigel loved so much, Gabe moved in slow motion, or at least it felt like it. Licking his lips, Nigel closed his eyes to savor the exact moment Gabe's soft, warm lips touched his. The movement was so wonderfully sweet, Nigel likened it to twinkle lights at Christmas. The beauty of soft little lights strung around an evergreen in the distance, dancing through the night sky filled with a gentle breeze pushing an incredibly piney and spicy smell to him, enveloping him in its comfort. In fact, that was what Gabe smelled like to him. Pine, clove, and orange like coming home for Christmas. Home. He was home.

He wrapped his arms around Gabe's neck, pulling himself up and closer to him. They were at an uncomfortable angle, but Nigel didn't want to break their kiss to adjust. He tasted coffee and cream with just a dash of sugar, exactly how Gabe took his morning coffee, and something else. Something inherently Gabe. His essence. And Nigel wanted to sip on that for the rest of his life.

But a knock at the window drew them apart so quickly Nigel's head spun. He was disoriented. Unsure where he was or what was going on. His body screamed at him to go back to kissing Gabe but one look out the window at Rhys, Kiter, Callum, Vidar, and Boyd, the last of whom was making kissy faces at them, Nigel knew their little bubble was broken.

Looking back at Gabe, pink cheeked and red lips, a sheepishly adorable look on his face, Nigel breathed a laugh.

"Well, we're never going to live this down," Gabe said.

"No," Nigel answered, grateful Kiter and Rhys herded Boyd away. He looked over at Gabe. "Are you all right? I mean you basically just came out."

Gabe took Nigel's hand in his and kissed his knuckles. "No more closet for me, baby. I want this. That good with you, Sweets?"

Nigel felt his face burst in a smile of sheer happiness. "Yeah, that's good with me. Can I ask... what changed your mind?"

"It's... complicated. A bit jealousy, a bit being hit over the head with it."

Nigel's brows furrowed. "Jealousy?"

"Yeah," he breathed a laugh. "The, ehm, headmaster asked if he could set you up with his nephew, or something like that and it just made me realize that you might want to date and even bring your date home, but I hated the idea of someone else touching you, kissing you, being in our space. It was the push I needed, I guess."

"Yes, the headmaster mentioned your reaction."

"He did?" Gabe's brow rose then he groaned. "What happened?"

"Nothing really. I tried to let him down gently. He'll bring his nephew to the game Saturday. I thought we could invite the team. The man only just came out and though his family seem supportive, he needs friends who have gone through what he's been through."

"You took him up on the date?"

"No," Nigel stated. "I told him I'm not available, but I'd be his friend. It was awkward enough knowing you nearly freaked."

"I didn't freak," Gabe shook his head. "I just came to a realization."

"Well, he knows I'm not interested so will you be nice to him on Saturday?"

"I guess I have to, huh?" Gabe asked. Nigel grinned and kissed his cheek.

"You'll be great, honey. Besides, if we bring Boyd, there won't be a chance for him to flirt with me."

"Ooh, harsh, baby. But brilliant."

"I know."

With that, they popped the doors of the car and got out heading up to their offices.

Chapter Nine

Nigel sat in the interrogation room on the third floor of the building. Rhys stood behind him, leaning his shoulder against the wall as they waited for Kiter to come back with Kyetti.

"So..." Rhys began.

"No," Nigel answered.

Rhys chuckled. "I was just going to say-"

"No."

"Oh come on," Rhys laughed. "I gotta know."

"Why?" Nigel turned to look at his friend, a smirk on his lips.

"Because," Rhys justified. "I've been with you since the beginning... sort of... and I feel like I'm on season three of this show and I can't stream it because I don't the live tele package."

Nigel chuckled. "What?"

"Come on, mate. I need to know."

Nigel sighed. "He made dinner last night for me and the boys."

Rhys' eyes grew wide. "He knows making you food is your love language, right?"

"I don't know but he also wore grey joggers and a white t-shirt."

Rhys groaned. "God, he'd look hot."

"He did."

"So that kiss?" Rhys asked. "Was it a thank you or something more?"

"Something more."

"And who initiated it?" Rhys asked.

"He asked this time. I agreed. And that was when you guys so rudely and lewdly interrupted us."

"Boyd interrupted. We stood by making sure he behaved," Rhys teased. "And let me just ask… did you kiss him back this time? Because it sure as hell looked like it."

Nigel gave him a cocked eyebrow and a look that said *duh!*

Before Rhys could answer, there was a knock on the door and Kiter appeared. Nigel sat forward and wiped the playful look off his face and replaced it with a blank stare as Kyetti shuffled his shackled feet into the room followed by two armed guards. Rhys stayed leaning against the wall giving the impression of indifference and calm but those who knew him, saw the barely contained, calculating martial artist beneath the surface.

Nigel had seen Rhys compete and supported him at his second degree black belt ceremony. He relaxed knowing if anything went wrong Rhys could take a pencil neck weakling like Kyetti.

Kiter took the seat beside Nigel and indicated the chair opposite him and the two guards pushed Kyetti into the seat. The once nearly elegant man, slouch and stared at Nigel.

"Mr. Kyetti, I am Director Scorpio, this is Agent Leo and I believe you know Agent Diamond," Kiter began. Kyetti said nothing just stared at Nigel. There was a pause of silence, then Kiter continued. "You are going to be arraigned on felony charges for your role in the trafficking, murder, and torture of hundreds of British citizens. In short, you're going away for a long time unless we can help each other. You help me, I'll help you. What do you say?"

There was a long pause, then, still without looking away from Nigel, Kyetti spoke. "I won't talk to you."

"Major Kyetti-" Kiter tried.

"Only to him," he pointed at Nigel.

"I'm afraid that won't be-"

"Fine," Nigel said. "With your guarantee that you will give us something."

"I think you'll want to hear what I have to say," Kyetti said.

Nigel glanced at Kiter. "It's all right."

Kiter looked between Nigel and Kyetti, then gave a nod. He stood and walked to the door followed by Rhys. Once he was behind Kyetti, the man spoke again. "And your guard dogs."

Kiter froze, his back going straight, and Nigel saw the subtle brush of Rhys' hand on Kiter's knuckles. Without words, Kiter knocked on the door and Gabe opened it. Nigel and Gabe locked eyes as everyone but Kyetti and Nigel left the room. Nigel gave Gabe a small nod and with a worried look on his face, Gabe shut the door.

They were alone.

At least, alone in the room. Nigel knew the guards were just outside and the team watched on the monitors in the other room close by. But alone or not, Nigel had a part to play.

"How are they treating you?" he asked softly. Kyetti stared at him. "If I asked them how you got that black eye and cut on your cheek would they tell me you fell down the stairs?"

"You were there. You saw."

Nigel remembered two days before when the team had captured Kyetti, Callum and Gabe were a bit heavy handed with their prisoner. Nigel looked down. "I didn't want them to hurt you."

"No?" Kyetti questioned sarcastically.

"No," Nigel kept his body language open. "But can you admit that what you've done to my people, if I would have done it to yours, our roles would be reversed and you would be treating me the same, if not worse?"

Kyetti was silent. Nigel sighed, stood, walked around the table, and leaned against it, crossing his ankles and arms as he looked down at the man.

"Look, I know it's easy to say from where I'm standing but I really do want to help you. You're a person no matter what you've done, and I want you to see that I mean it. And I know it's hard for me to see your side of things but if I can assure you of one thing it's this, if Director Scorpio says he can help you, believe him. He's a good man and I will ensure you get the best deal possible. But you have to help me, Anton. Give me something I can give to Scorpio." Nigel went quiet and waited. His background in interrogation techniques never came more in handy. *Make the person want to help you. Make them comfortable. The more dominate the person the more submissive you want to appear.* And most importantly, *be the quietest voice in the room.* So Nigel stopped speaking, allowing Kyetti to think. But when the silence lingered, Nigel switched tactics.

Sighed heavily, he stood and walked slowly toward the door. "I tried to help you. Remember that."

Just as his hand reached the doorknob, Nigel heard; "LOA Bank in Târgu Mureş. Vault 3962187. You will need 996519228 and SBV510877N,"

"Thank you," Nigel stated.

"And Agent Diamond?"

"Yes?"

"Come see me before I'm shipped off to god knows where."

"No, I don't think so, Kyetti. In my opinion you can rot in jail, and I hope the rats eat your face so no one ever has to look at such evil again." Without another word, he knocked on the door which opened just as Kyetti began to laugh.

"Be careful, boy. You know what happens to those who meddle? You don't want to be one of them."

"Threatening my people will get you no where, Kyetti," Kiter said, then motioned to the guards. "Take him away."

Gabe stood close and Kiter was on his other side. They walked in silence to the other room where Boyd, Callum, Marjorie, Vidar, and Leo all watched the live feed.

"Please tell me we got all of that," Nigel asked.

"We did," Callum confirmed.

"You were badass in there, mate," Boyd praised. "You really had him going."

"Thanks."

"You all right?" Rhys asked.

"Drained, but good." Nigel sat down. Gabe hovered around him. "So Romania?"

"Better," Callum replied. "Transylvania."

"Transylvania?" Boyd nearly shrieked in excitement. "Like vampires? Dracula? We're going to see Vampires?"

"Okay one, vampires don't exist," Kiter said. "And two there's a lot more to Transylvania than vampires, Boyd."

"Like... what?"

"Like the people, landscape, Medieval towns and architecture, churches, history dating back to pre-Roman times, a full and vibrant history, world renowned artists, musicians, and writers, not to mention a wealth of traditions, excellent cuisine, and of course plum brandy." Kiter smirked and glanced at Rhys clearly sharing a memory the rest were not privy to.

"Eh, sounds boring," Boyd sat next to Nigel. "I want to see the vampires!"

"You do know Father Christmas isn't real too, right?" Rhys questioned.

"Piss off," Boyd teased.

"Gentlemen," Marjorie stood. Her voice cracked and Nigel looked at her. She was a master at hiding her feelings but the subtle crack in the armor showed. For the life of him, he couldn't understand why something had rattled her. "Your tickets. You have a red eye leaving Heathrow tomorrow at 0600."

Nigel saw Gabe's worried look. It would be the first mission where the boys would be without Amelie to mind them. Nigel brushed Gabe's hand. When he looked down, Nigel gave him an encouraging smile.

"Gabe," Kiter spoke drawing their attention. "Why don't you take a few minutes to make arrangements for the boys. Or I'm sure Marjorie could help."

"Of course!" She offered. Whatever cloud had descended had vanished as quickly as it had come.

"Thank you, I'll just call my parents. They'll be able to take them for a couple days. I need to make sure they can do remote learning. They can miss a couple practices, but dad could drive them down for game. Will we be back Saturday, do you think?"

"Possibly, why?" Kiter asked.

"The boys have a game."

"And we wanted to invite you all because the headmaster's recently out nephew will be there, and he wants to set me up with him. I figured the man needs friends more than a shag," Nigel explained.

"I don't know," Boyd grinned like he smelled fresh meat. "I've been told I'm a fantastic... friend." He wiggled his brows suggestively.

"We'll plan on it," Kiter said with a nod.

"Give your dad my mobile number, if he needs any help, let me know," Marjorie's offered.

"Thanks."

"So, who's for some lunch?" Kiter offered sharing a look with Rhys who smirked.

Chapter Ten

Since HQ was closer to Heathrow than any of their homes, after Gabe got a boys settled with his parents that evening, he drove back to London and joined the team in the barracks. It wasn't fancy but it was comfortable. It was usually four to a room with bunk beds, but as the beds were fulls and not twins, Kiter and Rhys took a room alone with a queen bed. Boyd, Callum, and Vidar took the bunkbed room and Nigel and Gabe got their own room with two queen beds. Gabe stared at one of the beds with wonder and a little trepidation. He had never shared a bed with a man and never wanted to more than right then, but Nigel set his holdall bag down on the other bed.

"Better than some hotel rooms I've stayed in," Nigel teased.

"Yeah, same," Gabe turned away to look at the cinderblock walls and concrete floors.

"Did they say they'd have dinner brought in?" Nigel asked.

"Uh, yeah, I think so. Probably pizza."

"Sounds good. But not as good as your salmon."

Gabe smiled slightly and looked down. Nigel walked up to him. "Are you all right? You seem... off. Is it the boys? They'll be fine."

"It's stupid."

"It's not stupid. You're their father."

"I'm not thinking about the boys."

"Oh," Nigel's voice was a mixture of surprise and confusion.

Gabe sat on the bed in a huff. Nigel sat beside him, his pinky finger brushing Gabe's. "Then, what's wrong?"

"Why won't you share a bed with me?" He hated how petulant he sounded. He turned to look at Nigel when he hadn't spoken.

After a beat, Nigel took his hand. "Because I didn't want to presume. I never want to pressure you into anything. I don't want to ever make you uncomfortable."

"But I'm not. Not with you."

Nigel's smile lit his whole face and Gabe's breath caught. "Well then, okay. If you want me to share this bed with you, I will."

The butterflies in his stomach were new. "Can I kiss you?"

"You don't have to always ask. Consent is king, yes, but you have blanket permission to kiss me."

Gabe nearly lunged and Nigel laughed. But the laugh turned into a moan as Gabe swept his tongue inside Nigel's sweet sweet mouth. He had never felt better than he did at that moment.

They were sitting on the bed, but Gabe turned his body

and, leading with his torso, he gently pushed Nigel back until his head rested on the pillows. Gabe knew he couldn't be comfortable, bent at a ninety degree angle but for the life of him, he couldn't stop to adjust. There was a nudge on his lower stomach and he arched his back like a big cat. Nigel's left leg brushed underneath him never breaking their kiss. With a start, Gabe realized he was lying between Nigel's thighs. The man beneath him, and Gabe felt the *very male* part of him outlined beneath his trousers, was beneath him, legs spread to accommodate Gabe's hips, and it made Gabe see stars.

Nigel's moans as he gave his all to the kiss went straight to Gabe's cock filling it with need. Tentatively, Gabe lowered his hips to be flush with Nigel's. Their bodies met and he felt every inch of Nigel's erection. He moved, little gentle thrusts, rutting against Nigel, who gasped and moaned and kissed him. The sudden feel of Nigel's perpetually cold fingers lifting Gabe's shirt and digging into his back, caused Gabe to buck against him and break their kiss on a grunt.

Nigel locked his ankles around Gabe's hips and continued where Gabe had faltered. Thrusting his hips in short ever so tempting movements, Nigel kept his eyes locked on Gabe's and the intimacy of that was stronger than all the sex he'd had with women.

Gabe stared at the violet eyes of the man he loved. "Sweets," he moaned as Nigel's length rubbed against his. "I-"

"I know," Nigel replied, and Gabe felt those words to the marrow of his bones.

Slowly, Gabe leaned down, his eyes shifted to the bead of sweat sliding down his neck. Emboldened, he licked the streak and

Nigel bucked against him, moaning his name. Slipping his hands down beneath Gabe's waistband, he cupped his arse. The flavor of salt, musk, and his Sweets burst across his tastebuds and Gabe loved it. He leaned back down grazing his lips against the pounding vein under Nigel's jaw. Nigel hadn't shaved and the prickly feeling of his day-old scruff enhanced the heady sensations racing around him. He nipped at Nigel's neck causing his lover to cry out and dig his nails into Gabe's buttocks urging him on. The pain enhanced the pleasure as Gabe ran his tongue over the reddening pinch, soothing the sting.

"Gabe," Nigel gasped, then moaned.

"Nigel, I-"

The sound of a loud crunch, then chewing broke the spell, and Gabe's head whipped around over his shoulder. Their door was open, and Boyd stood, leaning against the jam, holding a bag of crisps and giving them both a shit eating grin.

"Please, don't stop on my account," he said.

Gabe grabbed one of the pillows and lobbed it at him. Boyd laughed and caught it. "Get out!" Gabe ordered.

"Buzzkill," Boyd teased turning from the door. "Kiter sent me to tell you pizza is here, but I'll tell him you already ate, shall I?"

"Asswipe!" Gabe yelled, then felt Nigel shaking beneath him. He looked down to see Nigel holding in his laughter.

"God, that kid has the absolute worse timing," Nigel said.

"I can't wait until he grows up. Maybe get a boyfriend of his own and we can repay the favor," Gabe grumbled.

Nigel's face went soft and Gabe felt the gentle caress on his back. "Is that what we are?"

"What?"

"Boyfriends?"

Gabe paused a long moment, simply rolling the title around in his head and heart. Both organs heartily agreed. "I'd like to be. If you're okay with it."

Nigel removed his hand from Gabe's back and cupped his jaw. "Yes, Gabriel Sebastian Collins, I will be your boyfriend."

Gabe's cheeks hurt with how wide his smile was.

"But please," Nigel went on, "one request."

"Anything."

"Don't break my heart because it will break me and there'll be no coming back from that."

Gabe moved his left hand across Nigel's chest and slid it over where he felt the strong steady pounding.

"This is safe with me, Nigel. I love you. And nothing will ever change that. You're my person. My *Sweet Caroline and good times never seemed so good.*" He quoted from Neil Diamond's famous song.

Nigel burst out laughing. "Oh, so original."

"Every word is true, Sweets."

"Who'd have believed you'd come along?" Sweets also quoted.

He leaned up and brushed his lips against Gabe's and sighed into the sweetness.

"Oh, sorry," a voice they weren't as familiar with said.

Breaking away, Nigel lowered his legs so Gabe could move, they looked at the door to see Vidar. "Didn't mean to interrupt," he said.

"No, no, we already were by Boyd," Gabe admitted and

rolled off the bed, standing to give Nigel room to get up.

"Yeah, sorry about that. Kiter wanted to let you know about dinner and Boyd volunteered, we tried to stop him but well... you know."

"Yep, we know," Nigel laughed.

"Thought I'd check on you because I know Leo has dietary restrictions but didn't know if you two did. Boyd's eating like there's no tomorrow."

"That boy, I swear. Where does he put it all?" Gabe asked as he and Nigel followed Vidar out of the room and down the hall.

"Can I ask... how old is he?" Vidar asked.

Gabe and Nigel shared a look. "Not exactly sure, he claims to be twenty-one, but I've never seen a license. Ask Leo. He'd know," Nigel replied with a smirk at Gabe's short laugh.

"Am I missing something?" Vidar asked confused.

"There's... history there," Nigel explained.

At Vidar's wide eyes, Gabe continued. "Short history, very short. One night stand sort of thing. No desire there at all. No BroCode breaking or anything like that."

Vidar went slightly pale and turned away from them. "I don't know what you're talking about."

Again, Nigel and Gabe shared a look. But Gabe couldn't help Vidar. The man clearly was attracted to Boyd, though the two men couldn't be more opposite. They'd be good for each other. Vidar needed to loosen up and live a little and Boyd needed to grow up a bit.

"There you are!" Kiter's voice called as they entered the room.

"The lovers emerge!" Boyd heralded waving a slice of

pizza in the air.

"Shut up, Boyd." Gabe and Nigel said good naturedly at the same time.

"You better have saved me some ham and pineapple," Nigel teased.

Boyd made a gagging noise and scrunched up his nose. "All yours, lover boy."

Rhys held out a medium pizza box. "Literally, all yours, Nige. None of the rest of us are insane. Pineapple doesn't belong on pizza."

"Agreed," Everyone else said.

Nigel shrugged. "There are two types of people in the world. Those who love pineapple on pizza and those who are wrong. Glad to know I'm on the right side of history." With a wink and a saunter that caused Gabe to clear his throat and adjust himself, Nigel went to one of the chairs and opened his pizza box.

"Delicious goodness."

Only after he turned did Gabe realize Nigel wasn't looking at the pizza, he was looking at him and the smile that lifted Gabe's lips was there for the rest of the evening.

Chapter Eleven

Nigel hated Gabe's alarm clock that next morning. Cocooned in the warmth and earthy scents of his... boyfriend, Nigel never wanted to leave the bed. However, Heathrow Airport waited for no man, the cheek, and their 0400 wakeup call was exhausting. But the quick make out session Gabe treated him to, tied him over as they hurriedly got dressed and ready to head out.

Boyd looked a little worse for wear as he trudged out of the room wearing joggers and a t-shirt, his eyes half opened and his hair askew.

Callum, Vidar, Rhys, and Kiter all looked as tired at Nigel felt as they all headed out to the car. Rhys packed everyone's holdalls in the boot and climbed in next to Kiter who leaned over to kiss him.

"All set?" Kiter asked.

"Aye, all good," Rhys answered.

Boyd let out a grumble as he leaned against the window and slipped in his earbuds, pulling the hood of his jumper and scrunched the material over his face. "Wake me when we get there," he said. "Or better yet, Thor can carry me and let me sleep."

Nigel watched as the newest recruit to their team blushed and looked away. He and Gabe shared a look and a smirk but the rest of the forty-five-minute drive was in silence until they parked. Checking in individually, they were ushered through security, and reached their gate with thirty minutes to spare until boarding.

With no one around yet, Kiter allowed them all to sit together. For security, they pretended like they didn't know each other. "Coffee? Tea?" Kiter offered.

"Oh dear god, yes," most of the men stated. Nigel sat beside Gabe as Kiter and Rhys headed to the coffee kiosk.

"You all right?" Gabe asked taking his hand.

Nigel breathed a laugh. "You always know when I'm thinking something, don't you?"

"I feel it."

Nigel smiled and leaned forward placing a quick kiss on his lips. Pulling back, he rested his head on Gabe's shoulder and sighed. "I'm just concerned. We don't know what is in the vault and if it was worth this trip. We also are no closer to finding the inside man who betrayed us killing our fallen brothers. And honestly, we don't have any proof there even is an inside man. I guess, I'm trying not to over think but it's easy to do in this case."

Gabe was silent for a long moment and Nigel was grateful he didn't just dismiss his concerns. But a part of him knew he wouldn't dismiss anything he said.

"You were in that room with KY. What does your gut tell

you? Do you think he was lying? Or perhaps stretching the truth?"

Nigel thought for a moment. "I do believe whatever is in that vault is important. But I don't know how important or how much will be useful. I do not believe he would give us anything to incriminate him, so I am intrigued."

"Intrigued is good." Gabe smirked and leaned over to brush his lips over Nigel's.

They heard a disgusted sound and turned, thinking it would be Boyd being Boyd, but instead of their teammate's laughing green eyes, they met displeased eyes of a woman in her mid-to-late forties looking at them as if they had begun to have sex on the airport floor.

"Can I help you?" Gabe questioned and out of the corner of Nigel's eye, he saw the other CCBoys, who had dispersed when more people arrived, subtly sit up and take notice.

"You should be ashamed of yourselves. There are children about," the woman spat.

"And god forbid they don't grow up to be as arrogant and bigoted as you," Gabe replied. "I shared a quick kiss with my boyfriend. It's not like we're copulating right here. How about you remove the stick up your arse and become a nicer human being."

"Don't you dare talk to my wife like that," the man spoke up and then proceeded to shout obscenities at them both. He called Nigel very unimaginative names for his race and their sexual orientation, and his stomach pitched as anger rose.

"Tell your wife to mind her own business," Gabe answered.

"You're disgusting! It's unnatural!" The wife screeched.

Gabe looked down at Nigel and his whole body shook.

Truth be told, Nigel was petrified the interaction would be too much for Gabe. Nigel was used to it. He bore the pain of being ostracized, having people see him and move to the other side of the street so they wouldn't walk past him, women clutch their handbags closer whenever he was nearby. He had been mistreated, spat upon, feared, beaten, but nothing, especially not Little Miss Bigot was going to make him change who he was.

"Ma'am, I'm going to ask you to stop," Kiter appeared next to the woman.

The man was in Kiter's face before Nigel could even blink. "Don't you dare tell my wife what to do!"

"Sir, calm down. We are in a public place," Kiter tried.

"Tell that to those two freaks! Making out in front of everyone! Have you no shame? Decency?"

"None," Gabe answered. "And we weren't making out. It was a simple kiss. I'm sure it's been too long for you to understand what that is."

"You little-" The man lunged for Nigel but he the next thing he knew, the man was on the floor crying and his wife was screeching. Nigel looked up to see Rhys in a relaxed ready stance next to him. He hadn't seen what Rhys had done, but the bigot was on the floor clutching his arm.

"You broke my arm!"

"I sprained it," Rhys answered. "If I wanted to break it, trust me, you'd have seen the bone."

"What's going on here?" A security guard appeared.

"I want these men arrested! They attacked my husband!" The woman cried.

The security guard looked at Nigel and his stomach

dropped. "Bethel?" He questioned. His and Gabe's former colleague at Scotland Yard, and the man who put Sweet in the hospital after beating him up in the locker room for being gay a couple months ago.

"Sweet?" Bethel's eyes landed on Gabe. "Collins?" Then he met Rhys' eyes and promptly looked away. "Boss."

"Bethel," Rhys stated. "This man was harassing Nigel, and..." he looked at Gabe. If he said the man was harassing them both, he would effectively out Gabe to another bigot. "And he started spouting off. He attacked Nigel. I nullified the situation. No one else needs to be involved. Just me."

Kiter stepped up beside his boyfriend. "Officer... Bethel," the way Kiter said the name made Nigel think he knew the history. "These men work for me and if I can speak with you privately, I can explain the situation."

"I already did, and he admitted to it!" The woman screamed. "I want them all arrested, dirty little freaks!"

"Ma'am, I'm going to have to ask you to keep your voice down, there are children present," Bethel said.

Nigel would have laughed at the karmic words had the situation not been so dire.

"It really doesn't matter what anyone says, mate," Boyd spoke up. "I got the whole thing on video." He held up his phone. "They were harassing my man here for being himself and when he tried to diffuse the situation, they reached for his man. Samurai over here took him out, *kachow!* And, mate, if that's how she feels about gay guys she and he deserved it. Not to mention what they called my friend here because of the color of his skin. Talk about bigots, I mean, man there's some horrible people in the world, but bullies, those who beat up someone for no other reason than they're different, that fucked up man."

"Boyd, shut up," Rhys ordered and with their nearly freaky ability to communicate without speaking, Rhys' eyes conveyed the situation. Boyd instantly shut up. Rhys and Boyd had become almost like brothers, which was weird to Nigel considering they had slept together nearly six months ago.

"I'm sorry," Bethel said softly drawing Nigel out from his thoughts. Nigel watched Bethel pull out his handcuffs. Sighing, Nigel stood, expecting to feel the touch of cold steel on his writs, but instead, heard the loud-mouthed protestations of the woman as Bethel hauled her husband to his feet and slapped on the cuffs.

Bethel locked eyes with him. "I'm sorry for what I did, Nigel. I was scared to come out and jealous of the open life you got to live. I took it out on you and can never forgive myself."

"Wait... what?" Nigel asked.

Bethel gave a sad smile and turned to Rhys. "You were right, boss. I was closeted. Majorly. But after what happened, I went to mandatory psych eval and was suspended. I'm still in therapy, but I've finally come to terms with being gay." He shrugged. "Got kicked out of the family, but I met an amazing man, and we've been together ever since."

"I'm proud of you," was all Rhys could say.

"Thanks," Bethel shrugged again looking shy as he looked back at Nigel. "I'm sorry I hurt you."

"Water under the bridge," Nigel promised.

"Thanks, let me get this guy taken care of." He stopped and turned back. "Could we have coffee? All of us? I'd like you to meet Matt."

"I'd like that," Nigel said, and Gabe took his hand. Bethel grinned seeing the movement and winked.

"'Bout time." With that, Bethel walked away lugging the man with him, followed by the woman screaming.

"What did you do, Somm?" Rhys asked Kiter beside him. Nigel looked over questioning.

Kiter shrugged. "You don't mess with my family and get away with it. I also have the full weight of the British government behind me. Your former Super is currently a nighttime guard at a mall and well, Bethel's psych eval wasn't good. I just happened to let it leak to the right people."

Rhys leaned in and whispered something to Kiter that made him laugh and kiss him. "Let's hope the rest of the trip isn't as... exciting," Kiter said to the team.

"But wait," Boyd piped up. "I don't get it. What and who just happened?"

"Come here, I'll explain," Rhys said as Kiter began passing out the coffees he had in the carriers.

Chapter Twelve

After a brief layover, they took a chartered jet and landed in Târgu Mureş airport. The layover in Bucharest was long enough, they were all able to freshen up and change into new clothes and have a bite for lunch. They had to break into couples with Boyd, Callum, and Vidar acting as businessmen traveling together. Their mission was too important, and their covers were too vital to risk someone knowing they were one big group. But when the chartered jet landed and they were the only passengers on the plane, they were able to meet up at the entrance of the airport.

"Did we rent a car, Scorpio?" Callum asked Kiter not wanting to call him *boss* in fear of prying ears.

"No, we're meeting a friend," Kiter replied cryptically.

"Ooh, a hot friend?" Boyd asked running his fingers through his hair, pinching his cheeks, and smacking his lips together.

Nigel watched Vidar's body language to see the man flinch and grumble, but he was too far away to hear what he said.

"Will he take me to see the vampires?" Boyd asked.

"Only if you ask nicely, малыш," a heavily Russian accented voice said to their right. The men stopped and turned.

Kiter grinned. "Sasha," he greeted him with an embrace and a slap on the back. "Good to see you, old friend."

"Mind that old talk, мудак," the man answered with a grin.

"You *are* older than me," Kiter replied.

"By two whole years, big deal," Sasha stated. Kiter laughed and patted the man on his back. Though the two years looked more like five to Nigel, he couldn't deny the man was gorgeous. He noticed Boyd and Callum nearly drooling. He stood just a little taller than Nigel's five-foot-ten-inch frame and was eye to eye with Kiter, but under the black Henley it was clear the Russian was well built. His arms were about the size of Boyd's thighs and the expanse of his chest had defined, if not large pecs, showing his physique. His legs were the size of tree trunks and his jeans slung low above a very ogle worthy bubble butt. His face was rugged with fine lines around his eyes and the lower half of his face was covered in a salt-and-pepper well-groomed beard. He wore a dark grey beanie hat on his head and a silver stud earring glinted in one ear.

"Two years, eleven months," Kiter spoke breaking Nigel's perusal of the bear in front of him. "But who's counting?"

"You apparently," Rhys said pointedly.

"Oh, baby, you know what I mean." Kiter winked. "Sasha, this is Leo, my... boyfriend."

"Leo?" Sasha questioned with a smirk. *"The* Leo?"

"The one and only," Kiter agreed giving Rhys a soft look.

"Huh," Sasha then said something in Russian that had Rhys chuckling and responding.

"You two can swap stories about me later," Kiter teased. "Let me introduce the rest of the team. Boys, this Oleksandr Demidov, affectionally known as Sasha. This is Fraxinus, our Ground Team Leader, Diamond," he indicated Nigel, giving their codenames. "His partner Reaper. Thor our rookie, and this is Autolycus, our thief and hacker."

"Ah, you're the one who wants me to take you to see vampires," Sasha said to Boyd.

"Daddy, you can *take* me anywhere," Boyd said, and Vidar made a coughing sound but Boyd ignored him.

Sasha smirked and motioned Boyd forward with two fingers. Boyd raced to stand before him. The differences in their build and height were almost comical. Sasha looked at him with an appraising eye.

"You like to be bitten, малыш?" Sasha asked.

Boyd licked his lips. "Anywhere, Daddy."

Sasha fought the smirk, then nodded once. "You'll be fun."

Boyd winked. "More than you know."

"Sasha, please, no flirting with my team," Kiter stated.

"No flirting, a promise," he winked. "Come let's get to van then we can talk more." He kept his eyes on Boyd. "Come with me, котик."

Following Boyd and Sasha, the team headed out of the airport. Nigel looked over at Gabe who merely shook his head and chuckled.

Sasha drove them through Târgu Mureş and about twenty minutes after they left the airport, he pulled the van into a car park. Once it was parked, he popped the door and everyone followed. They walked another fifteen minutes down alleyways and around buildings until they arrived at what looked like an old abandoned train station. The once beautiful Baroque architecture was run down and dingy. Parts of the roof had caved in and graffiti marred both the outside and inside.

No one spoke, though confused faces were bouncing around the team, apart from Kiter and Callum. Sasha approached a wall and pressed his finger to the exposed concrete. A digital panel popped out of the wall and Sasha typed on the keyboard and leaned forward for a scan of his eyes, then a beep sounded.

"Demidov, Oleksandr," Sasha said.

A voice came from a hidden speaker. "Agent Demidov, confirmed. Welcome, Agent."

Sasha stepped aside as a wall panel slid open revealing a revolving door. "Kiter, if you please," Sasha said indicating the control panel. Kiter stepped up to the keyboard.

"Each of you will type in your name, and the eight-digit code you picked when we left. Then, retinal scan, wait for the beep, and say your name, last, then first as Sasha did. Once confirmed, you will go into the body scanner and come out on the other side. Understood?" Kiter said.

"Me first," Boyd pushed ahead to the panel.

"Patience, my little зайчик," Sasha said. Then, with a wink, he entered the full body scan and disappeared past the door.

Boyd turned to Kiter. "He is gay, right?"

"No, he's Pansexual. He's a great agent and usually gets the marks, men or women, talking through BDSM."

Boyd groaned. "Let me through, boss. I'm ready to *talk.*"

Kiter chuckled and stepped aside. Boyd keyed in the panel, leaned in for the retinal scan, and the voice spoke again. "Agent Falstaff confirmed. Welcome, Agent." Boyd hurried to the revolving door and slipped inside.

"I guess we should probably destroy those no-fraternization docs when we get back to HQ, huh?" Kiter asked.

"It *is* a little hypocritical, babe," Rhys said.

Kiter shrugged but agreed and turned to Callum. Once everyone was through the revolving door, they followed Sasha down three flights of stairs to another door.

"Welcome to Târgu Mureş' Safe house," Sasha opened the door to an open concept apartment space. There was a kitchen, a large eating area, a living room with an eighty-inch television mounted on the wall, and multiple doors to their right leading to rooms with king size beds, plush looking pillows, and soft lighting.

"All right, boys," Kiter began. "Pick your rooms and get comfortable. The kitchen is fully stocked as per my instructions. Tonight is about relaxing. We'll brief in the morning for tomorrow's mission. Now, you've all been up since 0400, so feel free to go to bed whenever. Otherwise, there's beer, cold cuts, pasta salad, and everything else you could want in the kitchen. Gym is down the hall, pool and hot tub at the end of the hall. It's saltwater not chlorine, so no funny business. I won't be held accountable for cleaning, if you boys decide to fool around. Other than that, have at it."

Everyone headed down the hall to find their rooms. Gabe passed several until he found the last one. A king bed, dresser, nightstands, and a plush rug before an electrical wall-mounted fireplace. "This'll do." He grinned. He had plans that evening, even went to far as to grab some… necessary supplies at the airport gift shop. He walked in and set his holdall on the bed. Before he could do more than unzip it, there came a knock at the door. Turning, his eyes lightened on Nigel leaning against the doorframe.

"Hey handsome," he said.

"Nice room…" Nigel answered.

"It is, isn't it? And it's the farthest away from everyone else. Thought that might come in handy."

"Oh?" Nigel asked. "And why is that?"

"Well, I've heard a rumor that my boyfriend is pretty loud when he comes, so I figured best to be prepared," he winked and walked over to Nigel, taking him into his arms.

"You… want to have sex… here?" He asked.

The look in Sweet's eyes made Gabe pause. "Uhm, I mean… unless… you don't?""

"No, I-" Sweet started. "I just didn't realize you were ready to take that next step. It's pretty final when you do. I just don't want you having a gay freak out on me."

"I'm not going freak out and yes, I'm ready for that next step, if you are."

He waited an excruciatingly long time as Sweet debated. "Please don't take this the wrong way." Gabe's heart fell and his stomach twisted. "But I'm… not ready." Gabe swallowed hard and looked away. Nigel's arms tightened around him. "Please understand. I'm not rejecting you. I've wanted you for so long, but... we are on a mission. We need clear heads. And you only just started to realize your feelings, I want you to have time to think about this. It's not something to take lightly, my love. Once we do this, that's it. No going back. You're it for me."

"And you're it for me."

"Am I though?" He questioned. "How do you know? You've only been with women. You love me, yes, I have no doubt. But I don't want you to rush into this. Come out to the main area, have a beer with me. Let's be with our teammates and hold me tonight when we go to bed. But let's not take such a big step tonight, all right? Please understand."

Gabe took a breath and nodded. "I do. And you're right. It's just, I've been confused for so long and now that I know what I want, have come to terms with what I am and who I want, I don't want to wait. But you're right. Maybe we can plan for it when we get home."

"Let's think only for the now," he said. "I know how much I want you. I'm just worried. It's a big step in our relationship. If you hate it, I don't want you to leave me. I'm scared of that, Gabe."

"Hey, don't be," he hugged him tighter and placed Sweet's head on his shoulder. "I love you and that will never change."

Nigel buried his face in Gabe's shoulder and with soft strokes, Gabe soothed his hand up and down Nigel's back. They stood there for a long moment, then Gabe pulled back slightly, and Nigel looked up at him with those unnerving, violet eyes and Gabe leaned down. Their kiss was soft, gentle, loving, and it was everything Gabe needed and wanted. A reassurance that Nigel was his. His Sweets. His. The man he loved was in his arms and no one could hurt him or take him away.

They broke the kiss and after a beat, rested their foreheads together. Their breath was quick but not labored as they took each other in.

"I love you, Nigel," Gabe said softly.

Nigel smiled and Gabe felt his thumb stroke the back of his head. "I love you too, Gabe. With all my heart. I always have, I always will."

"And as far as not liking sex with you? Perish the thought," he grinned. "I can't get enough of you." Nigel breathed a laugh.

With one last kiss, they parted and held each other's hand as they walked to the doorway. Vidar and Callum passed them with a nod, one heading to the pool, the other to the gym.

"I should probably get a workout in too," Gabe said.

"If you want, but I'd rather lounge with you in the hot tub later tonight."

Squeezing Nigel's hand, he smirked. "I'm not paying for cleaning, so we'll have to be good."

"No promises," Nigel winked as they walked out to the main area. The tele was on and Rhys and Kiter were in the kitchen, the smells of something wonderful filling the air.

Chapter Thirteen

"Oh! Nah! That's cheating!" Boyd cried as Rhys showed his full house, ace high, poker hand winning the pot... again.

Everyone else around the table cried out in dismay as Rhys raked in the earnings. Not that they were playing with real money, just some chips they found in the poker set in the entertainment cabinet.

"Seriously, boss," Callum said to Kiter as he took a swig of his beer. "You giving him some of your cards?"

"Yeah," Gabe chuckled. "No man is that lucky."

"I will ignore the fact you blamed me, Cal. I am innocent in all this. I'm losing just as much as you," Sommerset claimed.

Rhys leaned over and kissed his boyfriend's cheek. "Don't worry, baby, you'll get lucky tonight."

The men around the table hooted and hollered giving wolf whistles as Rhys captured Kiter's lips and Kiter leaned in, deepening the kiss.

Sasha said something in Russian that caused Rhys to laugh and break the kiss.

"Ugh, I need a cold drink after that," Boyd teased and stood. He wore a pair of tight leggings coming to his mid-calf and an oversized sweatshirt that fell off one of his slim shoulders as he stood. He walked past Sasha who reached out and smacked Boyd's ass, hard. The kid squealed and giggled.

"Get me one too, малыш," Sasha ordered.

"Yes, Daddy," he grinned and sashayed to the kitchen.

Sasha watched him go and adjusted himself vulgarly as a salacious grin lifted one side of his lips. "One more game, gentlemen. I have an arse to claim soon." Sasha drained his beer.

Of course, Vidar took that moment to come into the room, sweaty from his workout. Nigel saw the pain cross his features when he heard him. "You shouldn't speak about him like that. He's not some property," Vidar said.

Sasha leaned back in his chair and looked at Vidar. They stared at each other for the longest time. "What right do you have to tell me how I can and cannot speak about him?" Sasha demanded in a voice so cold it made the hair on the back of Nigel's neck stand on end.

"Well, I-" Vidar stammered then looked helplessly around the room. "I..."

"As I thought, you have none." Sasha turned back to the game and the room was silent.

"I don't like it. He shouldn't be an object. You speak of him like he isn't... isn't..." Vidar was floundering. Nigel wanted to help but couldn't. It wasn't his fight.

"Isn't what?" Sasha asked. When it looked like Vidar couldn't think of anything to say, Sasha snapped his fingers and Boyd walked over to him having heard the entire conversation in the open concept kitchen. Sasha slipped his arm around Boyd's hips, squeezing his ass.

"Малыш, now do you want to be treated like demure lady like this хуй is suggesting? Or a whore like I want to treat you?" Sasha looked at him expectantly.

Boyd's reaction was not what Nigel had expected, what he had hoped. Boyd looked up at Vidar then down at Sasha. He slipped his fingers across Sasha's scalp revealed by the short buzz cut and smirked. "Well, I'm no lady and I don't like to be demure. So, Daddy, I think I'll stick with being your whore."

"That's my good little boy." Sasha gripped Boyd's ass.

"In fact," Boyd slipped to his knees between Sasha's legs and cupped the sizable bulge. "I'm pretty needy right now, Daddy. Do you *have* to play another hand?" Boyd's hand rubbed Sasha's groin and the Russian chuckled then leaned forward.

"Get naked and get in bed, in that order, малыш. Daddy'll be right there," Sasha said. Boyd grinned and bounded off toward his room without a glance at Vidar when he passed him. Sasha took a long swig of his new beer Boyd had brought him, emptying half the contents down his throat in one go. He sucked his teeth, then stood. "Deal me out of next hand. I have ass that needs spanked and very eager boy to please." With that, he sauntered away and as soon as he passed Vidar, he paused. "It's cute you think you have chance with him. Why don't you go find yourself nice, innocent girl and settle down? You're clearly not ready for this life." He took one step then stopped again. "Oh," he turned to him once more, his voice that cold tone that made Nigel shiver. "And if you challenge me like that again, I won't be so kind."

He then glanced toward the others in the room and raised his voice as he wished them good night in Russian. Entering the room, he disappeared but his voice drifted down the hall. "Good boy, Daddy likes it when you follow instructions."

"I'm nothing if not a pleaser, Daddy," Boyd said next just before Sasha shut the door.

There was a long pause then, Rhys spoke. "Vi, come on over, we'll deal you in."

"Yeah," Nigel agreed. "It's just for fun. We can play whatever you'd like."

It took Vidar a moment but soon, he took a deep breath and looked up, flashing a smile. "Thanks, but I'm beat. I'm going to turn in."

"Vi," Rhys tried again when Vidar turned away and shut the door to the room next to Boyd's.

"Shh shh," Kiter tapped his boyfriend's hand. "Let him be. There's nothing we can do."

"He shouldn't have to suffer like that," Nigel stated.

"No," Kiter agreed. "But he also shouldn't have challenged Sasha."

"Oh come on," Rhys looked incredulously at him. "If the guy I was about to sleep with talked about me like that in front of you, how would you feel?"

"That's completely different," Kiter said.

"Is it?" Rhys questioned.

"Yes, one, they're not together and Sasha is a very... different type of person. He doesn't like being challenged and he takes what he wants."

"Still no excuse, boss," Nigel said.

"I agree, but there's nothing to be done," Kiter replied.

"Oh my god," Rhys shook his head.

"What?" Kiter asked.

"You've slept with him yourself, haven't you?" Rhys stared at him.

Kiter opened his mouth to speak, then closed it on a huff. "It was a very long time ago. My first trip to Russia."

"You're unbelievable," Rhys shook his head and got up from the table.

"Babe," Kiter followed him into the kitchen.

Callum, Gabe, and Nigel looked at each other awkwardly. "Well, on that note, I'm going to turn in," Callum said.

"Yeah, I think it's about time to get to bed," Gabe agreed. "Good games though," he said as they all stood and gathered their things.

"Yeah, fun," Callum agreed. "Have a good night."

"You too," Nigel called after him. Then, lowering his voice, he spoke only to Gabe. "He so... mysterious. I'm so curious about him. Is that weird?"

"Who? Callum?" Gabe asked. Nigel nodded. "Not at all. He's our leader and we know very little about him. Makes for difficult trust issues. But I can't say I wouldn't act the same if I were Team Lead. There's a type of aloofness needed, I guess."

"I suppose." They walked back to their room hearing the grunts and moans coming from Boyd's room. "Poor Vidar." Nigel shook his head. "Walls aren't thick enough for that sort of noise. And he's next to them!"

"He'll be okay." They reached their room and closed the door. They could barely hear the sounds drifting down the hall. "Maybe this will make him step up and admit how he feels. It's scary, I know."

Nigel wrapped his arms around Gabe's waist and stared into his grey eyes. Gabe instinctively wrapped his arms around Nigel too. "You above anyone would know, baby. I'm so proud of you."

He grinned and kissed the tip of Nigel's nose, pulling him close. They stayed like that, embracing for a few minutes before Gabe pulled back.

"I was going to call the boys before they get to bed," Gabe said.

"Of course," Nigel grinned. "Give them my love."

"Stay. I'm going to video call Hunter. They'll want to see you."

Nigel's smile widened and they sat on the bed together as Gabe pulled out his phone and brought up his eldest son's number.

Chapter Fourteen

Gabe woke that next morning happier and more content than he ever felt, just holding his man to him. He lay on his back, Nigel's head resting on his chest, his arm flung over Gabe's stomach and his ankle locked with his. Gabe tightened his arm around him and leaned down kissing Nigel's tightly curled black hair. He buried his nose taking a deep inhale and smiled.

"Did you just sniff me?" Nigel's groggy voice asked and Gabe silently chuckled.

"Beware, I may mark my territory too what with Sasha around."

"Not into water sports, love. I've already been peed on once before in my life, not something I'd like to do again." Gabe stiffened. He hadn't meant to remind Nigel of that time with the bullies. Nigel moved his head so they could look at each other. He folded his hands together and rested his chin on his knuckles. He smiled faintly at him. "Baby, don't. I was teasing. Besides, I think I already smell like you."

"Good," Gabe said and leaned down to kiss him. There was no tongue as he was well aware of Nigel's dislike of morning breath but the dazed look on his face when Gabe pulled back made something inherently male, puff up his chest. "Good morning."

"Mm, morning," Nigel replied. "Don't suppose there's any coffee?"

"Probably. Want me to go check?"

"Yes and no. I'm comfy, but I need coffee," Nigel said.

Gabe chuckled as Nigel stretched his lithe body alongside him like a cat.

"What's more important? Me or coffee?" Gabe asked.

Without hesitation, Nigel said, "coffee."

"I'm hurt, baby," Gabe chuckled.

"Sorry," Nigel patted his cheek sleepily. "But if you want me to be any good on the mission today, I need coffee."

With a soft kiss to Nigel's forehead, Gabe got out of the bed, giving Sweet a look when he yelped and quickly covered his bare torso with the blankets.

"What?" He questioned. "It's cold!"

"Poor baby," Gabe teased and pulled on his grey joggers over his briefs and grabbed a white t-shirt. "I'll be right back."

Nigel moaned when he saw him but nodded. Gabe had the distinct impression he was staring at his ass as he left, and he liked it.

Waking up for the second time with Sweets wrapped in his arms was becoming addictive. He had a chance to talk to the boys the night before and they both were as happy to see Nigel as Gabe expected. They chatted to him like he was a second father and it warmed Gabe's heart to hear his sons say *love you both* when they hung up.

The kitchen and rooms were quiet as Gabe found the coffee machine and some ground roast in a vacuumed sealed bag. As he measured out the coffee, the door to Boyd's room opened and he glanced up to see Sasha leaving the room then turned back to Boyd who appeared in nothing but an oversized white t-shirt. Sasha wrapped his arms around Boyd's waist and pulled him in, giving him a hungry kiss. Gabe looked away. He and Nigel had switched rooms with Vidar halfway through the night and had heard enough sex to last them a long time. The coffee began to brew and Gabe focused on that. When the kiss ended, Gabe glanced up to see Boyd watching Sasha walk down the hall. He then turned to Gabe and grinned.

"Coffee, yes, the elixir of the gods," he said and sashayed over to the kitchen island waiting for the pot to finish brewing.

"Thanks for the porno last night," Gabe spoke. He meant it to sound teasing but it came out with more bite than he had intended.

Boyd gave him a confused look. "You were down the hall. Didn't think we were that loud."

"We switched rooms with Vidar."

Boyd stared and blinked at him owlishly. "You were next door? Why?"

"Didn't think it was wise or fair to force Vi to have to listen to your orgasms all night long. What are you doing, Boyd?" Gabe asked.

"Don't know what you mean,"

"You know exactly what I mean. That man adores you. Worships the very ground you walk on, and you can't be bothered to give him the time of day. Trust me when I say this. He's not going to wait around forever."

"There's the no fraternization policy. Stupidest thing I've ever heard but there it is. Doesn't seem to effect you and Sweet or Rhys and Kiter but that's my luck, huh?"

Gabe shook his head and poured three cups of coffee. Boyd swiped one and fixed it with sugar and cream.

"It's not fair to him," Gabe tried again.

Boyd shrugged. "Not my problem and not yours either." He turned and headed back to his door. Then looked back at Gabe with a mean smile. "And by the way, Collins? You might want to think about your own man instead of mine. He's not gonna wait around for you either. It would be just terrible if someone stole him from you."

"Go ahead and try, you little shit," Gabe said with only a little heat. "I know where his loyalties lie. Can you say the same?"

Collins took the two mugs of coffee and walked around a stunned Boyd to the room next to his. Sweet looked up from the bed and smiled softly. He had adjusted so his back rested against the headboard. Collins climbed over to sit beside him and handed him one of the mugs.

"What was that all about?" He asked.

"Sorry you had to hear that," Gabe took a sip of his coffee. Sweet waved him off and waited expectantly. "Just Boyd being Boyd. I was trying to get him to stop treating Vi like he is and he threatened to try to take you away from me."

Sweet chuckled. "As if he could."

"That's what I said."

Sweet took Gabe's hand and held it tightly. "You're it for me, Gabe. And you were just trying to help a friend. Vidar is lucky to have you. As am I, as is this whole team."

Gabe gave a small smile and looked up from where their fingers intertwined to stare into his eyes. "I love you."

Sweet's smile took his breath away. "I love you too."

They drank their coffee sharing soft stories of the boys when Kiter knocked on the open door. "Briefing in twenty."

"We're ready, boss," Gabe replied.

"Good, Rhys is making some breakfast for us. Come on out whenever."

Sweet rested his head on Gabe's shoulder. Gabe smiled softly and rested his head on Sweet's. They said nothing for a long time until Nigel asked a question, very softly. "If Amelie begs for you to come back to her, promises to make it work. Will you go back to her?"

Gabe tensed and Nigel pulled back to look at him. His handsome face so open and concerned it tore at Gabe's heart.

"To be completely honest with you, I haven't thought about it. I want to say no but you deserve more than an emotional answer. So baby, I can't say."

Nigel swallowed hard and closed his eyes. "Thank you for being honest with me."

"I'm sorry."

"For what? You told me the truth. That's all I could ask for." Nigel paused, took a breath and kissed his cheek before getting out of bed. "Come on, I smell food."

Gabe didn't move immediately and watched Nigel leave

the room. He was alone. He knew something was bothering Nigel last night. Gabe hadn't lied to him. Couldn't lie to him. He hadn't thought about what he'd do if Amelie reached out. She was the mother of his boys. For their sake would he... try to make it work? The mere thought made him sick. But for their sake... no, he couldn't.

His phone buzzed on the nightstand, and he grabbed it, seeing a text from his dad.

Dad: Papers have been served. I requested all communication be made through your solicitor ie., me. The formal writ for custody for H&C has been filed. Stay safe.

Gabe: Insomnia still got ya, dad? It's, what, 0500 over there? But thanks.

Dad: 0530, but what can I say, old habits and all that. I was in the gym every day at this time.

Gabe: Show off

His dad sent back a gif of Taylor Swift singing *Haters' Gonna Hate.* Gabe chuckled and replied with Iron Man's eye roll and a laughing emoji,

Gabe: When I get back, we're going to have to have a serious discussion about your gif skills. A 68-year-old man shouldn't be using TSwift.

Dad: 67... and anyone can love TSwift. Come on now, don't be ageist, son *Winky Emoji*

Gabe chuckled and replied with;

Gabe: Whatever old man, gotta go.

Dad: Again with the age... watch it with the old, boy. You're not too old to take you over my knee.

Gabe: I'm so scared.

Dad: You should be *Laughing Emoji* Be careful, love you

Gabe: Will be and love you too.

With that, Gabe turned his phone to sleep, took his coffee, and headed out to the living area nearly running into Vidar, looking freshly showered and wearing jeans.

"Hey, mate," Gabe greeted. "You look more rested than last night."

"Yeah, cheers," Vidar said. "I appreciate it."

"No worries, happy to help."

"Coffee, lads?" Rhys called.

"I'll take a top up," Gabe said.

They headed over to pour a cup and Gabe's eyes caught Sweet's. The poor man was getting the rapt attention of Boyd Falstaff. Clearly, the boy thought he had a chance with following through on his earlier threat. Sweet rolled his eyes causing Gabe to chuckle. But when Boyd put his hand on Gabe's man's shoulder, something snapped and he stalked over, swiped Boyd's hand off Nigel's shoulder, clasped the back of Sweet's neck, leaned down, and fused his lips to Sweet's. His Sweets. Nigel kissed him back and grasped the back of his head holding him in place. Long enough but too short at the same time, Gabe pulled back winking at Nigel as he sat beside him.

"Right, while Leo is finishing up breakfast for us, which smells lovely, let's start," Kiter began.

"Was that little show of possession really necessary?" Nigel whispered leaning into him.

"Yes," Gabe answered.

Nigel shook his head, an amused look on his face as he leaned back and focused on Kiter.

"This bank is old, but the technology is the best the east has to offer. Here's the plan. Leo, Sasha, you're Beta Team. You go inside as a distraction. Thor and Reaper, you're Charlie Team. You will pose as Texan Oil Barons who have a meeting with the bank president. Sasha has the name."

"*Da*, a Mr. Dascălu," Sasha said.

"Boyd, I need you to hack the email system and set aside a meeting time, so it looks legit," Kiter went on.

"Easy," Boyd began typing.

"At the right time, Leo you cause a scene. My thoughts are, Reaper or Thor you ask for a cup of coffee and once the person goes to get it, Leo jostles the coffee to where she spills it all over you. Reaper, you need to ensure she leaves the lobby and that you exit. During which time, Boyd and Fraxinus, you're Alpha Team, you slip in and get to the vaults, here. We," he motioned to Sweet and himself. "Are Foxtrot team. We are in the van watching and guiding the whole way. Boyd, you'll need to tap the main line on the communications box, so we have access to the CCTV feed. We'll look at it from the van."

"Not difficult," Boyd winked at Sweet. "I'm multitalented."

"Once you get the contents of the vault, Boyd and Fraxinus exit through the fire escape here, triggering the alarm and vacating the building. Everyone meet back at the van a kilometer down the road. This isn't a game, lads, you know that. But we can do this as a team. Let's get ready," Kiter stated.

Once they had their assignments, they went back to their rooms to change. Suits for Vidar and Gabe, jeans for Rhys and Sasha. And black sweaters, black pants for Boyd and Callum. Each man was outfitted with body cams and the link uploaded to the internal server. Callum received two guns from the weapons cache and Boyd tinkered with a device to hack into the cameras.

With a breath, Kiter gave the expected pep talk, and they were on their way.

Chapter Fifteen

Kiter pulled the van down an alleyway two kilometers from the bank. Kiter and Sweet climbed into the back of the van and with a kiss to their men, the doors opened, and the other six men stepped out and shut the door behind them. Sweet turned to the monitors and watched as Boyd and Callum hurried across the street and down another alley then across one more street to the alley entrance they needed. Callum stood watch beside Boyd as he pulled off the cover to the electrical hub on the side of a brick building. They were silent as Boyd worked the fiber cable up into the piping and guided it to tap the mainline for the CCTV inside and outside the bank.

"Scorpio, check." Boyd was looking down at his tablet where he could see the interior of the bank.

Kiter clicked on the keyboard next to Sweet and the snow cleared on the monitors as the camera feed pulled up.

"Affirmative, Autolycus, we have visual. Looping feed now." A few more clicks on the keyboard and Kiter spoke again. "CCB cameras looped, it's a go, it's a go."

"Affirmative, Scorpio, Charlie Team closing in on target in thirty seconds," Gabe announced.

"Confirmed, thirty seconds, Charlie Team. Come in Beta Team?" Kiter asked.

"Scorpio, this is Leo, Beta Team knocking at door," Rhys' voice came next.

"Affirmative, Leo, be safe," Kiter said.

"How do you do it, Kiter?" Sweet asked, muting his comm.

"Do what?"

"Let the love of your life go into these situations without being by his side?"

Kiter was quiet a long moment. "By living everyday like it's our last."

"Foxtrot, this is Charlie, in position. Knocking on door." Gabe sounded confident and Sweet swallowed down the bile that filled his mouth. He should have been beside him. He needed to be beside him. But, they had two separate duties.

"Good work Charlie Team. You are meeting with a Mr. Dascălu," Kiter said.

"Understood," Vidar replied.

"Alpha Team, two minutes?"

"Confirmed," Callum answered.

"Beta Team, Charlie Team, you have ninety seconds."

For the next thirty seconds, Sweet heard Rhys and Sasha speaking in Russian at the teller counter getting more and more agitated. Building up to the distraction. Gabe and Vidar were greeted by the employee nearest the doors as expected. She spoke in Romanian and Gabe looked over at Vidar confused.

"Sorry, darlin'," Gabe gave a convincing Texan accent. Then, did what nearly every stereotypical American would do, raised his voice and spoke slower. "You. Speak. American?"

The woman blinked and forced a smile on her face. "Yes, I speak English, Mister..."

"Oh, that's real nice. Name's Marsden, little lady, and this here is Jim Stewart. We got a meetin' with a Mr. Dask-aloo about some investments."

"I'm sorry? I don't believe Mr. Dascălu has you on his calendar." She walked back over to her desk and sat down pulling up the calendar.

"Definitely check that out, sweetheart, we spoke with a Mabel. Was it Mabel, Jim?"

"Believe so," Vidar answered in his near perfect Texan accent as well.

"Why wasn't I picked for Charlie Team, boss?" Sweet chuckled. "You should hear my Texan accent."

"Unfortunately, there is a reason beyond your control."

Sweet nodded sagely. "Gotta love my skin color. Opens so many opportunities." He didn't think he could sound more sarcastic or roll his eyes any harder. Kiter shrugged sympathetically.

"We don't have a Mabel here, gentlemen," the bank employee was saying.

"You sure about that? I remember distinctly because my momma, god rest her, was Mabel-Lynn and I don't forget that name."

"Could it have been Marlita?"

"Nah, I told y'all it was Mabel."

"I'm sorry, sir... oh," she must have found the meeting on the computer. "I do apologize. I do see your meeting."

"Now, see I told you. And it was Mabel who set it up, wasn't it."

She gave a tight smile. "Of course."

"Ha, see Jim. Told ya."

"Mr. Dascălu is ready for you, if you'll follow me."

"Before we do that, darlin'," Vidar began. "Could we get some coffee? I don't know what time y'all call this, but in Texas it's the ass crack of dawn and I can't function without some coffee."

"Make it two, sweetheart," Gabe said and tapped her on the behind as she walked past him.

"Of course," she said tightly.

"Thank ya kindly," Gabe answered winking.

"Good job, Charlie Team, Alpha Team standby for go sign," Kiter said.

"I'm seriously going to have to de-misogynize myself after playing this character," Gabe grumbled.

"Not a word, babe," Sweets said.

"Yeah it is. It is today, anyway."

Sweet chuckled.

"Thank goodness you're gay now," Boyd said over comms. "The population of women is saved."

"Enough out of you," Gabe replied.

"CCB, focus. Beta Team heads up, she's on her way back."

On screen, Sweet watched as Rhys and Sasha began yelling and gesticulating. Rhys aimed one wild arm just right and knocked the poor woman in the back jostling her and catapulting her and the hot coffee straight into Gabe's chest. He thanked his lucky stars his boyfriend had a couple layers underneath his pristine white shirt so the burn wouldn't be bad.

"Alpha Team, go go go," Kiter ordered.

"Whoa there, missy, you all right?" Gabe asked her.

"Oh, Mr. Marsden, I do apologize," she said.

"No harm done," he replied. "Don't you worry your pretty little head about it. Ain't nothing that can't be fixed."

"It burned you?" She asked.

"It's a little hot, but so's the Texas sun, sweetheart and you don't see me complainin' about that, now do ya?"

"No?"

"No is right. Now how 'bout you run along and get yourself cleaned up. Mr. Dask-aloo can wait a few minutes."

"Oh no," she shook her head. "Elena can take you in," she offered.

"All the same to you, sweetheart, I like you better. Go on now, and we won't say a word to Mr. Dask-aloo about it. Blame it on me, darlin'."

"You are sure?"

"Surer than a bet on a horse named Devil in the Texas Rodeo while listenin' to George Strait. Now, you run along. But don't be too long. We're likely to miss ya."

"Thank you." She turned and left the area.

"Well done, Charlie Team. Exit when convenient. Meet at rendezvous in ten. Alpha Team status?" Kiter asked.

Sweet looked over to their cameras and wasn't surprised to see they were in the building and down the second flight of stairs leading to the basement with the vaults."

"At vault door, Scorpio," Callum said. "It's a keypad. Autolycus."

Boyd moved into position to hack it. "We got a problem."

"What is it?" Kiter asked.

"It's a scramble code. Means it's going to take a long time to crack. If I don't have the exact nine-digit number to open the door, I won't have it until New Years'. It's a scramble," Boyd said, then turned to Callum. "Just blow it."

"Too risky," Callum denied.

"Wait," Sweet said. "Nine digits. Autolycus, numbers and letters or just numbers?"

"Just numbers."

"Our window of opportunity is closing rapidly, Boys. If you have something Diamond now would be a good time to say it." Callum spoke.

"Try... try this," Sweet prayed he was right. "996519228."

"Niner-niner-6-5-1-niner-2-2-8," Callum repeated, and Boyd keyed it in. The red light turned green. "We're in."

Sweet let out a breath and Kiter thumped him on the back. "Good job."

With a nod of thanks, they watched as Callum and Boyd hurried down the steps and hallway to the vaults.

"Bingo." Boyd cried eureka and the vault in question showed on their body cams.

"Confirm vault number 3-niner-6-2-1-8-7," Callum requested looking at the vault.

"Confirmed vault number 3-niner-6-2-1-8-7," Kiter said reading the numbers.

"Autolycus," Callum gave the go ahead.

"Code," Boyd requested.

"Sierra-bravo-victor-5-1-0-8-7-november," Sweet said as Boyd keyed in the code and the lock disengaged.

Slowly turning the crank, Boyd opened the vault door. Immediately, red lights flashed, and a siren screeched. They had tripped the alarm.

"Son of a bitch," Kiter pounded on the counter. "Alpha Team, abort."

Callum ran to the main vault door that was closing and held it open. "Autolycus, retreat," Callum shouted grunting as he held the door back with all his might. "Now, dammit."

"Got it." With that, Boyd raced toward Callum and slipped through the opening. With a grunt, Callum followed and let the door shut with a resounding clang.

"Sus mâinile!" Voices of the guards shouted and Sweet saw the men, guns drawn aiming at Callum and Boyd.

Callum was saying something to the guards, but it was drowned out by their shouting. Though Sweet didn't know the language, he could surmise it consisted of "on the ground!" "hands up!".

"Beta Team, get out of there," Kiter ordered. "Rendezvous in five minutes." With no reply, Kiter whipped off his headset, placed the earbud in his ear, and climbed into the driver's seat. "Hold on." He tossed over his shoulder to Sweet.

Eyes fixed on the screen Sweet saw Callum and Boyd on their knees as the guards kept shouting at them, then suddenly behind both guards, Rhys and Sasha appeared, incapacitating them without hesitation.

"Alpha Team and Beta Team extracting," Sweet called to Kiter.

"Thank fuck," Kiter mumbled. "Hold on!" Sweet did as Kiter took a particularly sharp turn on nearly two weeks. "Shit, we need a getaway driver. Diamond, give me status."

"Charlie Team in position in two, Alpha and Beta eta seven minutes. Coming in hot," Sweet gave him an update.

"Shit." Kiter touched his ear. "Fraxinus, come in."

"Read you, Scorpio," Callum sounded out of breath as he ran.

"Status?"

"Three bogeys behind, hear multiple sirens. No injuries to report. ETA five minutes give or take a firefight."

"Do not engage, repeat do not engage. Get to Extraction Point B."

"Negative, Scorpio, path unavailable, trying to shake."

Kiter's breath went shaky. "Leo."

"I know, Scorpio," Rhys said. "We're going to be fine." Then a shot rang out and Kiter nearly lost control of the van. The commotion on the other side of comms was so chaotic, Sweet could barely follow.

"Diamond?" Kiter demanded.

"Lev, Lev's hit," Sweet said. Lev, Sasha's codename meaning Lion. "Fraxinus and Leo returning fire."

"Status?" Kiter demanded.

"Flesh wound," Sasha came over the comms. "I'm fine." In the camera, Sweet saw him shake off Boyd who was trying to help. "Get to extraction point."

Kiter maneuvered the van down the alley they had picked

for extraction. Gabe and Vidar already in position. Sweet opened the door and they climbed in quickly. Sweet locked eyes with Gabe relieved he was safely inside the van. Gabe grabbed the military grade weapon Vidar offered and they took up position on their stomachs side by side, the guns' stands steadying them. They hooked their feet into the netting behind the front seat as a makeshift seatbelt in case Kiter took off quickly.

"Coming in hot," Callum shouted.

"We have you covered, Frax," Gabe said just as the four-man team appeared around the corner, running like hell followed them.

"Diamond, with me," Kiter called and Sweet climbed over Gabe to slide into the front seat.

"On my mark, Scorpio," Vidar called.

"Affirmative," Kiter said, eyes on the rearview mirror, hands on the steering wheel, van in gear ready to peel away.

The sound of the weapons firing behind him made Sweet's ears ring, but he trusted their aim, both the best shooters on the team. Boyd jumped in followed by Sasha.

"I hate shooting cops," Gabe muttered after he let off another round. Sweet noticed they were both aiming at arms and legs instead of torso.

"Leo!" Callum shouted behind him turning and firing at the police behind him. "Come on!"

"Go! I'm right behind you," Rhys shouted having fallen behind. Sweet's old boss and dear friend had injured his back and leg when in the military, but he was still running as fast as he could. It wasn't fast enough.

"Leo!" Gabe shouted as Callum jumped in.

"Come on, baby," Kiter murmured.

Sweet glanced at him, his jaw set firmly, then heard the shouting and shooting around him. And looking in the mirror, he saw it. Rhys stumbled as one of the police shots ricocheted off the wall spraying brick debris into his face. In that split second, Nigel made his decision. He wouldn't let his friend fall behind. He popped the passenger door and grabbed his sidearm.

"Diamond!" Kiter shouted.

"What the hell are you doing?" Gabe screamed at him, but he ignored it, racing toward Rhys firing as he grabbed his arm.

"Eejit!" Rhys spat. "What do you think you're doing?"

Sweet threw him unceremoniously into the back of the van and climbed in taking Boyd's seat as the younger man climbed into the passenger seat.

"Go, Scorpio," Vidar shouted, and Kiter didn't hesitate. The van peeled away as the two sharpshooters covered their exit. Once they turned a corner and were clear for a few seconds, Gabe and Vidar grabbed the rope next to them and tugged the doors closed. No one spoke, the van heavy with silence, apart from everyone's labored breathing.

Sasha was cleaning his wound and Rhys used a small mirror to dab at the scratches on his face that the shrapnel had caused.

They lost the tail somewhere along Strada Tofalau and Kiter pulled off onto Strada Terebici and crossed the river twice before he pulled off on a dirt road, leading to nowhere. But soon a small shack came into view and Kiter pulled the van into the rundown garage. The van was in park with the engine off.

The cabin quiet, then, "what the hell do you think you were

doing?" Kiter demanded turning and pinning Sweet with a hard glare.

"I-" Sweet started.

"All of you," Kiter's restraint on his barely controlled anger slipped as he turned in his seat. "Boyd, when your team leader says abort, you run like hell and abort. And Rhys," his breathing turned ragged as he looked at his boyfriend. Kiter didn't speak, clearly seeing the resignation in Rhys's eyes. He instead turned to Sweet. "And you, jumping out and going against direct orders."

"Saved him, didn't I?" Sweet demanded.

"You could have gotten both of you killed," Kiter shouted.

"But I didn't and you're welcome by the way. You still have a boyfriend thanks to me."

"That wasn't the plan. God dammit, every time. Every fucking time something goes wrong. Can't we just work together as a team and do one goddamned mission right?" Kiter popped the driver's side door open and got out slamming the door as he left. The team took a collective sigh.

"Let him cool down. Lester was breathing down his neck at HQ before we left," Rhys revealed. "He's frustrated and scared and when he gets like that he likes to flex and lash out. He'll be fine. Let me talk to him. Get Sasha inside."

"I'm fine, flesh wound. It's already stopped bleeding," Sasha revealed.

"Is this safe house like the other one?" Boyd asked softly.

Rhys nodded and placed his hand on Boyd's shoulder squeezing in comfort. Boyd handed his messenger back to Callum as he shuffled to get out. "I got the contents of the vault. But I think there were two codes. One to get in and one to raise the alarm.

Kyetti gave us the latter. Nothing we could have done." He shrugged slightly. His lips screwing up on one side, emphasizing his words. Boyd slipped to the end of the van and opened the door. "Sorry I'm such a disappointment."

"Boyd," Rhys sighed but Boyd left and walked toward the cabin, arms around himself. He had hunched in and looked so young, so frail but Sweet knew better than most, beneath that frail façade was a strength that baffled all who knew him.

Vidar got out next and hurried to him. Sweet watched as Boyd flinched when Vi reached for his arm. Vidar said something but Boyd shook his head. Stopping to watch Boyd walk on to the house, Vidar waited. After a few steps, Boyd turned back and gave Vidar a small smile and his lips moved saying *thanks.* Vidar nodded once then, waiting until Boyd got inside, he turned and stalked into the woods.

"Excuse me while I go yell at my boyfriend," Rhys huffed then looked back at Sweet and squeezed his forearm. "Thank you, Nigel for coming back for me."

"Always, boss," Nigel promised.

Sasha was next out of the van leaving Sweet and Gabe alone. They said nothing for a long minute, then Sweet forced Gabe's arms apart and crawled into his lap, wrapping Gabe's arms around himself without words. Gabe gave a sharp sigh but rested his head on top of Nigel's and tightened his arms around him.

"When you jumped out of the van," Gabe broke the silence after a moment. "I literally saw my life flash before my eyes. I saw my world darken and I was helpless to do anything about it."

"I know," Sweet muttered into his neck.

"No... no, Sweets you don't know." Gabe moved and

pushed Nigel back slightly. They locked eyes and Nigel's breath caught when he saw the look in Gabe's eyes. "I love you. I love you more than life, and my one thought was, if you died out there, I could never tell you. You are my world. You and my boys. Our family. You are my life. My heart beats in time with yours. And if yours stopped beating, so would mine. I love everything about you, Nigel Sweet from the way the little divot appears between your eyes and how you stick out the tip of your tongue always on the right side of your lips when you're thinking too hard. I love how you give your all to any project you are passionate about. I love you aren't afraid to live true to who you are. I love how kind, gentle, and loving you are to everyone but especially to Hunter and Colton. I love how happy you make me just knowing you."

He cupped Nigel's face and Sweet felt the dampness on his cheeks. "But most importantly, I love you. All of you. And I want you to know, nothing, and I mean *nothing* and *no one* will ever come between us. Yes, I may need to talk to Amelie again if she tries to reach out, but hear me loud and clear when I say this, Nigel. You are the *only* person I want forever with. And I will spend the rest of my life proving that to you. There is no one else for me but you. I love you with all my heart, soul, and mind. Sweets, be mine. Be with me. Let me prove to you how much I love you. Let me make love to you."

"I love you, Gabe Collins. I have since I first heard your voice calling off those bullies seventeen years ago. I love your boys like they're my own not just because they're yours but because they are wonderful boys and will grow up to be amazing men like their father. I want to be with you, more than anything, but I need to make sure you understand what you're asking. I'm no prude and I hook up, no strings, that's just sex, just scratching an itch. With you, it would be heart and soul so if you have any doubts tell me now. I'm not a woman. Sex between two men is different. I'm happy to be your teacher but you need to know, I'm all man. There's no boobs, no wet pussy. Just me, my ass, my hard body. Can you handle that?" He was being vulgar pointedly.

"I don't want a woman. I want you and only you. Will you show me how?"

Nigel heard and felt Gabe swallow hard after his confession. He took a moment to let the reality settle over him. His best friend, the man he always wanted but never thought he would have, wanted him. And he was cutely nervous about it. Nigel let the happiness of the moment flow through him, and he grinned as he cupped Gabe's face. "There's nothing I want more than to make love to you."

Gabe paused for a moment, then lunged forward capturing Nigel's lips with his. Nigel wrapped his arms around Gabe's neck and deepened the kiss. He felt the love and passion only deep friends turned lovers could feel and it lit a fire inside him.

Pushing away panting, he loved what he saw mirrored in Gabe's flushed cheeks, dilated glazed eyes, and lazy smile.

"I'm not doing this in a van that smells like body odor and blood," Nigel teased.

Gabe groaned. "So high maintenance." Grinning, Gabe released him, and Nigel didn't waste any time. He grabbed their holdalls stashed under the seats in the well and hurried out of the van. They raced into the house laughing as they made their way to the exposed brick wall. After they entered their code and were scanned, they raced down the cement stairs to the safe house below. They passed Sasha drinking a beer alone on the sofa.

"Want a third?" He called after them, a teasing lilt in his tone. They ignored him and nearly collided with Callum coming out of his room in gym shorts and a cut off t-shirt. They threw a *sorry* over their shoulders and tuned out Callum's indulgent chuckle as he shook his head.

Finally, they reached the last room and raced inside. They didn't take in the room apart from the queen-sized bed in the middle of the back wall.

The door shut behind them and Gabe locked it, then met Nigel in the middle of the room. Teeth clacking in the force of their kiss, Nigel's grabby hands went to Gabe's shirt and tugged at the hem. Breaking the kiss long enough to get his shirt off, Nigel took a step back just to look at Gabe. He had seen him shirtless, even naked in the locker room more times than he'd admit but that time he was able to actually look. And he looked his fill.

Gabe was built like a linebacker. His obliques were defined but his abs were more like a box with less definition. His pecs were large with dusty rose-colored nipples peaking under Nigel's scrutiny, and Nigel wanted to run his tongue in the deep valley between them. His shoulders and arms were a thing of beauty. Defined, thick muscles corded down the length of his arms bunching and releasing as Gabe twisted his shirt in his hands.

His chest was nearly devoid of hair, but Nigel bit his lower lip seeing the bit of hair trailing down and disappearing below his waistband. Nigel itched to touch the soft, hot looking skin. But before he could, Gabe caught his hand and, with a sexy grin, he spoke low. "Your turn."

The butterflies in Nigel's stomach fluttered their wings as

he took hold of the hem of his shirt and pulled.

The expanse of chocolaty skin being revealed inch by torturous inch to Gabe, made his mouth water and his hands itch. Gabe had seen him shirtless, hell even naked and he had snuck little glances every time he walked by, but to be given permission to look, to touch, kiss, worship, was a heady sensation and it raked a chill down his spine settling in a delicious heat pooling in his groin.

Nigel was fit, in a trim runners' physique. His chest and stomach were flat with a tempting line down the middle bisecting his torso. His chocolate-colored nipples were covered in a slight dusting of curly black chest hair that extended across his upper chest and down the bisected trail disappearing beneath his trousers. The definition of his shoulders and arms with sinewy muscles running the length, thin but strong made Gabe want nothing more than to feel those arms around him.

"You're beautiful," Gabe sighed and breathed a laugh when Nigel looked away shyly. He stepped forward and reached out to him, eyes asking for permission.

Nigel took a step toward him and pressed against his outstretched hand. His skin was warm, the hair springy and prickly at the same time and as Gabe rubbed his calloused hand across Nigel's chest, he reveled in the groan his Sweets gave him.

"I can't believe it's taken me this long." With furrowed brows, Gabe concentrated on the feel of Nigel's body. He heard every breath, every bitten off groan, every soft sigh. His hands covered that part of his chest where his heart pounded beneath his fingertips like a drum beating in time with the conductor. Gabe felt that same beat in his chest and as Nigel reached up to touch him, his hand covering Gabe's heart, they locked eyes realizing their hearts beat as one. And with a jolt, Gabe knew he never wanted his heart to beat even once out of sync with Nigel's. They were one.

Holding Nigel's gaze, Gabe licked his dry lips and took a breath as another realization dawned. "I don't know how to do this. I mean, I do, but not... I don't want to hurt you."

Nigel cupped his face. "You won't."

"Teach me?" The soft smile that lifted Nigel's lips made all the strong parts of Gabe go... gooey.

"Always," Nigel whispered, then, taking his hand, he backed up against the bed.

Sitting, he reached for Gabe's belt and loosened his trousers. Without hesitation, Gabe shucked his clothing watching Nigel do the same. Sweets leaned back on the bed, his hands flat behind him on the mattress, and looked up at him.

"Come to me," Nigel said and that did it for Gabe. As he slowly crawled up Nigel's body, and onto the bed, kissing his way up Nigel's torso, he hovered over the man he loved. For the first time in his life he didn't want to just have sex, he wanted to make love. He wasn't in lust with Nigel as he had been with all the women he had been with. He was in love for the first time in his life.

"Show me what to do."

"Find the lube in the drawer," Nigel said and indicated the nightstand. Gabe leaned over and opened the drawer. He found a small bottle and pulled it out along with a condom packet.

"How much do you know about gay sex?"

Gabe shrugged. "I watched some porn."

"When?"

"A couple nights ago. I never came so hard."

Nigel chuckled. "Well, let's try to remedy that."

"Yes please." Gabe looked at the bottle of lube in his hand. "I need to stretch you, right?"

Nigel nodded. Without another word, Gabe popped the lid on the bottle and poured some of the lube onto his fingers. Locking eyes with Nigel, he nearly swallowed his tongue when Nigel lifted his legs and grabbed under his knees. Eyes zeroing onto his hole, Gabe, tentatively at first, circled the pucker with one finger before slipping inside to the first knuckle. Nigel breathed out on a soft moan and Gabe loved the sound.

"That's it. Just like that," Nigel praised as Gabe moved his finger in and out. "Add another."

With his other hand, Gabe grabbed Nigel's calf and kissed his way up to his knee. His two fingers never faltering their rhythm. Licking his way, he sucked a bruise onto his inner knee nipping at the skin and slipping his hand up higher to Nigel's thigh.

"Fuck," Nigel groaned. "Add a third baby."

Gabe did but lunged forward to capture his moan. Working his three fingers in and out of his best friend, nothing ever felt better, and he knew besides the birth of his boys, this day would go down in history as the best day of his life.

"Fuck yes. That's it, baby. I'm ready. I can't..."

Gabe crooked his finger and found the area he was looking for.

"Fuck fuck fuck!" Nigel whimpered as he toyed with it. "Yes! How.... How did you?"

"Please baby," He scoffed. "I may have only just discovered this side of myself, but one thing I know is, there is nothing quite like prostate stimulation. Even straight men like it. I'm a huge fan."

Nigel looked up at him and grinned. "I'll be happy to explore that later."

"You better."

"Shit. No more. I'll come if you do. I want you inside me."

Gabe swallowed down his trepidation. Nigel was right, this was a big step for him. He'd never been with a man and though it was Sweets. His man. He still didn't know what to do besides the obvious.

"Hey, you with me, Gabe?"

He nodded. "Just nervous I'll fuck this up."

The corner of Nigel's lip tipped up. "We could fuck up or down or sideways, baby. I've wanted you since you protected me from those bullies. I've dreamt of this moment for nearly twenty years."

"I'm sorry I was such an idiot and didn't see you."

"You saw me. Or you wouldn't be here. I wrote you the week after my 18th birthday and told you how much I love you."

Gabe looked up. "The letter you told me about?"

Nigel nodded.

"I didn't get it, baby. I wish to god I had."

"You weren't ready then. And had you been, you wouldn't have those amazing boys. We're where we need to be now. I love you."

"I love you. So much."

"Make love to me, Gabe. I want to feel you fill me up."

With a swallow and a short nod, Gabe tore open the condom packet and rolled it down onto his length. Panic flared as he felt his size and remembered how small Nigel's hole felt.

"I promise, it's okay," Nigel said. "You'll fit."

With a breath, he notched the head of his cock at Nigel's entrance. They locked eyes again and Nigel nodded. Slowly, tortuous and delicious, Gabe inched forward reading Nigel's face, knowing every expression. When the ring of muscle gave way, and he slid all the way in, Nigel gasped, and Gabe paused. He tried to ignore the incredible tightness and heat surrounding him, but he couldn't.

"Fuck," he moaned. "You feel incredible."

"Move Gabe, I'm okay."

"Are you sure?"

"Oh yes, I need you."

Gabe pulled out nearly all the way and slowly slid back inside. Their mutual groans echoed in the room. Before he picked up the pace, Gabe slipped his hand across Nigel's chest to where his heart pounded beneath his fingertips.

"I love you, Nigel Sweet. I love you so much."

"I know, Gabe. I love you too."

With that promise, he picked up the pace and watched his lover come apart beneath him. His orgasm building at the base of his spine, he waited and angled so he could hit that sweet spot inside him over and over again. After what felt like forever and yet, hardly anytime, Nigel let out a gasp followed by a moan and his channel gripped Gabe so tightly, he couldn't hold back. He let go and flew to the highest point knowing his man would catch him.

He was in love, and he made love to the man of his dreams, slowly, passionately, feeling his heart next to his, feeling his body accept him inside, his gasps, his pants, his groans, his release. It was perfect.

Nigel Sweet was his in every way, in all ways, forever.

Chapter Sixteen

The flight back to London the next morning was quiet.

After saying goodbye to Sasha at the airport, they landed about three hours later. Nigel wanted to take Gabe's hand. He wanted to walk with him, show the love he felt, but they all had different seats and weren't supposed to look like they knew each other as they got off the plane to rendezvous at the van Marjorie waited in. He saw Rhys and Vidar making their way behind him and felt Gabe's eyes on his back. The night before had been... incredible. Making love to Gabe was the single most perfect thing Nigel had ever felt in his life. They held each other after, spoke low, confided things, told each other they loved each other and though he was going on only two hours of sleep, it was worth it just to finally have his man.

Gabe hadn't needed much teaching and Nigel enjoyed every second of Gabe's newfound excitement.

Kiter hadn't spoken to anyone other than Rhys and to say goodbye to Sasha. Same with Boyd. The team dynamic was off. But after stopping off in the restroom, Nigel found the nondescript van and knocked the code. He climbed in and was pulled directly into Gabe's chest. He sighed. He was home.

"God, I missed you," Gabe murmured in his ear. "You were sauntering that sexy ass in front of me, and it took all of my considerable will power not to join you in the loo."

Nigel nuzzled into Gabe's neck and hummed happily. "I felt your eyes on me and had to make sure I kept your attention." He grinned.

"If you are going to kiss, I would suggest doing so now. More boys incoming," Marjorie said from the front seat.

"Can't go against orders," Gabe teased and captured Nigel's lips with his.

After far too short a time, they were forced apart by a knock at the door. Opening, Vidar climbed in and sat opposite them. He nodded once and gave a short smile but said nothing. One by one the CCBoys arrived at the van and climbed in. Last of the group was Kiter who took the passenger seat next to Marjorie.

Without words, Marjorie put the van into gear, and they were off back to HQ. The tension in the van nearly ruined Nigel's good mood... nearly. But sitting beside his boyfriend, their fingers linked, and a soft smile lifting their lips was more than he could have dreamt. He felt more like a teenager with his first big love and all the sappiness it brought with it and not the thirty-three-year-old man he was.

Once they were underground in the parking garage, Nigel expected something to happen. It was as if the van and everyone in it was a bottle of Cola and the events leading up to that moment and all the emotions running around the team were Mentos being dropped into the bottle and they were waiting for the explosion. But nothing happened. At least nothing until they reached their floor and the briefing room, the lecture style room was cold and dark after a few days of disuse.

Kiter flipped on the lights and walked to the front as the rest of his agents entered and took a seat. All expect Boyd.

"Well," Kiter began after a deep sigh. "Hello."

"I have something to say," Boyd spoke up. All eyes turned to him. He looked... apathetic.

"Please, if I may go first," Kiter began.

"No, no you may not," Boyd went on. "You can shut the fuck up and listen for once. I am sick of you treating us like we're children. Like we're goddamn expendable. Like we are idiots who don't follow the rules you set out and then break yourself. I am exhausted keeping up with your mood swings, your attitude, and how you handle things. We didn't screw up on this mission no matter what you think. We followed protocol, we fulfilled our side. It wasn't our fault Kyetti gave us bad intel. It wasn't our fault the alarm went off. But instead of treating us as equals, as field agents, you go off on us like naughty little children. I'm sick of it. If you had asked or even listened, I would have told you what happened, but no. Hear me now, loud and clear, if something doesn't change, I'm done. I'm done with this whole fucking place."

Boyd was panting after he spoke, and Nigel couldn't fault him. Everything he said was true. And as the team looked at each other, apart from Rhys, they all shared the same look. Boyd was right.

Nigel looked over at Kiter who had locked eyes with Rhys. They seemed to be communicating in that freaky way all couples did. Gabe grabbed Nigel's hand and squeezed.

"You're right," Kiter finally said. "And I'm sorry." They waited as if expecting something else to happen. Kiter took another deep breath. "I behaved abysmally, and I have nothing left to say but I am sorry. You risked your life to get us the contents of that vault. And Nigel you risked your life to save Rhys. I..." he swallowed. "I don't want to lose anyone else on this team. We already lost so much, and it scared me when I could do nothing. I don't want another mission to be a failure because of me. You all deserve better than me. So after this case is closed, I'll be tendering my resignation for field work and appointing Callum as Deputy Director with Rhys as Team Lead in the field. I will be here behind a desk handling the day-to-day functions of the team."

"No," Callum stated. "No," he said again, then stood up. "So you got heated, you were scared. We've all been there. Boyd, need I remind you of how you reacted when Darius and Hesler were killed? This man has the weight of our entire department on his shoulders. Not to mention our lives and he strives to stay impartial but hell, we've all gone through a time where we lose it. Need I remind you this is the same man who went to bat for us so we could keep our jobs? The same man who was willing to take the blame for a botched mission. Try to imagine it this way, you already lost two men because someone inside your organization wants to end your team. You don't know who. You don't know why. And then the break you might need is overshadowed by the possibility of messing up again. If it wasn't clear before, it is now. Someone wants your team dead. So I think the man, who is human, is allowed to be upset. We all messed up but we're all here now, alive. And if that's not enough, I say this," he turned to look at Kiter. "You leave, I leave."

"Cal," Kiter breathed. "I can't allow that."

"That's the deal. You saved my life; you got me out of the shithole. I'm with you, always. You know what you mean to me. And it sure as hell is more than some fucking job," Callum revealed.

Nigel had never heard Callum speak so much in one setting. It revealed a lot about him and yet said nothing at all.

"Look," Boyd continued. "I don't want you to resign. I'm just asking for a little respect. Treat me, us, like equals. Yes, you're our boss, but you don't own us."

Kiter looked over at Boyd then locked eyes with each of the team members. "I promise this, so long as you're my team, I will do everything in my power to treat you as my equals. In many ways, you are my superiors, but I love each and every one of you." He glanced at Rhys. "Some a little more than I should and in a different way." Rhys smiled at him. Then, he turned back to the team. "Can we all go on from here? I will do everything I can, but I also need you all to focus and no more going against direct orders. I don't care how important the information was or is, you are more so. And I don't want to lose any of you."

They nodded and murmured their agreement. "Thank you, it is more than I deserve." Kiter nodded once to Boyd who sat beside Callum. Then, a pause and Kiter was back in command. "All right, CCB Team," he turned to the screen behind him and opened his laptop then handed packets of papers to Rhys who stood and passed them around. "These were found inside Kyetti's safe. I

147

emailed them to Marjorie who printed out multiples. Boyd, there's a microchip with your pack. It's encrypted, according to my intel."

"On it," Boyd pulled out his tablet.

"The rest seem to be ledgers of some kind written in a type of code. We need to decode this. And fast. So any suggestions?" Kiter asked.

Everyone studied the pack in silence apart from Boyd who was typing on his tablet.

"Can it be that simple?" Vidar breathed.

"Vi?" Kiter asked.

He looked up and saw everyone staring at him. "Uh, sorry. I think... it's a PigPen Cipher."

"A what?" Nigel asked.

"It couldn't be that simple, could it?" Callum stated.

"Well, I mean, it's a simple cipher but it's not one anyone does anymore. It's like the VIC Cipher, it's pen and paper. Everything is digital now. I doubt the younger generation even knows what it is," Vidar said.

"It's a Tic-Tac-Toe cipher originated in the 1700s by Freemasons. It's a geometric simple substitution cipher." All eyes turned to Boyd after his offhand comment. He hadn't looked up from his tablet as he kept typing.

"Ehum... yeah, he's right," Vidar said.

"Wikipedia is my friend," Boyd teased, and the team chuckled. "What? Ol' man over there dissed my generation. I had to stand up for us. Gotcha," he winked.

"Care to explain, Vi?" Kiter offered the podium. Vidar looked over at Callum who motioned his head.

"It's your discovery, go on."

With a nod in thanks, Vidar headed to the front of the room and took one of the dry erase markers. "A PigPen Cipher is, like Boyd quoted from the internet, a Tic-Tac-Toe cipher, but with a twist. It has variations for each letter of the alphabet. So, in the first nine squares you can see it is just like a Tic-Tac-Toe board and in each space you put the first nine letters of the alphabet: A-B-C-D-E-F-G-H-I. Then you create another board and continue with: J-K-L-M-N-O-P-Q-R. However, with this board to keep it separate from the first one, you place strategic dots inside the boxes. First row dots are placed at the bottom inside corners for J and L and the bottom middle for K. Then middle row the dot is on the middle side for M and O and middle bottom for N. Then for the last line the dots go at the top inner corner for P and R and top middle for Q. For the last eight letters you draw two large Xs and fill in S-T-U-V starting at the top then the two in the middle and finishing with V at the bottom. For the second X, fill in W-X-Y-Z the same way as the first X, starting with W at the top, X and Y for the middle and finishing with Z at the bottom. Then you add a dot to each inner corner for the second X only. Thus giving you distinct compartments for specific characters." He moved to the free space on the board and began drawing box symbols. "With that as your cipher, you can write a message."

"What does it say?" Boyd asked.

"You tell me," Vidar grinned. "Look at this symbol. It looks like an uppercase L correct?" Boyd nodded. "So find the correlating box on the cipher that looks like an uppercase L with no dot. What do you find?"

"C," Boyd said.

"Correct," Vidar wrote C inside the L shape. "This one?" He

pointed to the backwards L shape.

"A," Nigel provided.

"And this one?" Vidar pointed to a full box with a dot at the bottom.

"N?" Boyd asked.

"Yes, and of course that spells C-A-N. Next?" Vidar took them through the short four-line message he had written on the board which spelled out:

C-A-N

Y-O-U

R-E-A-D

T-H-I-S

"Cool," Boyd beamed nearly bouncing in his seat. Vidar gave him a shy smile.

"Do you really think it's something so simple?" Rhys asked. "I mean not to shite on the parade here or whatever, but I doubt Kyetti would have something that simple encoding his documents."

"How do we know these are Kyetti's documents? He knew the vault codes, but he didn't say anything about this being his. We said give us something. He gave us something," Gabe offered.

"And nearly got us killed in the process," Boyd grumbled.

"I'll be having a little talk with Kyetti, don't you worry. But for now, this is at least the first wall we can jump. Vidar, good work. I'll leave you to lead the translation. I want as much of this as possible done today. Boyd, I know you have my company credit card memorized by now-"

"Had it the first time I used it, boss," he interjected.

"Figures," Kiter rolled his eyes. "Order pizzas or curry,

whatever the boys want and get some beers in here. It's going to be a long night. Collins, you need to call your boys?" Kiter asked.

"Around 2100 if that works, boss, before bedtime," Gabe said.

"No problem. Sweet, with me. Kyetti won't talk unless you're there."

"Probably won't talk with me there. I burnt that proverbial bridge."

"Still want to have you on hand," he said. "Marjorie, with me. Have at it boys, and order whatever you want." Kiter headed up the stairs.

"Order me a coconut curry, will you?" Nigel asked Gabe before placing a kiss on his lips.

"Sure, be careful."

"I will." Nigel stood and followed Kiter out of the room. "You sure about this?" He asked.

"No," Kiter answered and let Marjorie stop at her desk to call down to MI6's holding cells. After confirmation Kyetti would be there, Nigel, Kiter, and Marjorie headed to the elevators.

Chapter Seventeen

The knock at the door broke the silence that had stretched as Nigel waited with Kiter in the interrogation room.

"Play up whatever angle you want," Kiter muttered.

"Be angry," Nigel said and watched as Kiter's face morphed. On cue, Nigel let tears fall from his eyes and covered his mouth. He had always had the ability to cry on demand and it worked in their favor. He nodded to Kiter who called out telling the guards to come in. As soon as Nigel saw Kyetti, he let out a sob and Kyetti's mouth quirked up.

"Sit down," Kiter ordered.

"I'll stand, thanks," Kyetti said smugly.

"I said," Kiter kicked the chair out hitting Kyetti in the balls. "Sit. Down."

The guard forced him into the chair as he whined and tried to cup himself with his cuffed hands.

"You've got some nerve," Kiter spat. "You sent my team into unknown territory and gave us bad intel."

Kyetti's face screwed up into an evil, strained grin. "Had some trouble at the bank did you?"

Nigel whimpered and looked away. "You son of a bitch," Kiter exploded. "You gave us the alarm code. The whole building was locked down and the firefight to get out-"

"You took something from me," Nigel sobbed. "You took the only thing that meant something to me."

"No hard feelings," Kyetti said. "But an eye for an eye?"

"What's that supposed to mean?"

"I told you to be careful. I told you not to meddle. I warned you not to get on my bad side. You didn't listen." Kyetti shrugged.

"I hate you."

"Now now now, it's just business. Nothing personal. If I had met you before all of this," he lifted his hands and the shiny silver bracelets around each of them. "You would have made us millions. You have the looks and the knowledge. But you chose the good path. In your mind, I am bad and that's all there is to it. But gentlemen, I'm just a businessman."

"The deal we discussed is forfeit," Kiter said. "You gave us nothing. You cost agent lives."

He grinned again. "Do you honestly think I trusted your *deal?* No offense, but you have a terrible poker face. Târgu Mureş was my insurance policy."

"Yeah? Well, we got the contents. Our agent sacrificed his life to get it to us," Kiter said and Nigel whimpered appropriately as he watched Kyetti's body language. He shifted in his seat. There was something in that safe he didn't want them to get.

"You will find nothing connected to me," he said.

"Maybe, but we have the best codebreakers and hackers this side of the pond. We'll reach out to Langley if ours can't break it. We'll find something and when we do, you're never going to see the light of day," Kiter replied.

"Oh, I will see the light of day very soon, Director. You're not the only ones with friends."

"I guarantee the sun will super nova before you see it again."

"So poetic," he teased. "I'm surprised you don't write a book; *How to be Tedious, a Life Memoir.* I wouldn't expect it to be very long but it could be a bestseller."

Nigel looked at Kiter. "I want to be alone with him."

"Not happening," Kiter replied.

"I need it. Please," he said. "No cameras, no audio, no guards. Just me and him."

"Diamond, no," Kiter answered.

"Do this, for me, for him," Nigel placed his hand on Kiter's forearm and Kiter stared at him trying to communicate.

Are you sure you want to do this?

Yes, trust me.

Kiter took a deep breath and stood. "Goodbye, Major Kyetti," he said. "I don't expect we'll meet again."

"Oh we will, Director, you can count on it."

With that, Kiter left the room grabbing the guards with him. Kyetti and Nigel stared each other down, not speaking until they heard Kiter's voice on the intercom. "Cameras and audio cutting in three-two-one." The sound cut out and Kyetti smirked.

"Who was it? Your lover? The youngest on the team? The

most to lose? Who died?"

Nigel took a couple shallow breaths and let another couple of tears slip down. He wiped them angrily and looked at him. "You disgust me."

"You're entitled," he nodded.

"But," Nigel said through clenched teeth and glanced at the two-way mirror then moved so his mouth was turned away from the wall so no one could read his lips. "I admire you. You keep calm. You're seven steps ahead of us. You're playing 3D chess, 4D even. And you don't let anything phase you. How?"

Kyetti shrugged. "People I know."

"But how did you get him to tell you about our missions?" Nigel was playing with fire, and it could go either way.

Kyetti stared at him. "I don't know who you mean."

"Yes you do, don't give me that."

"What assurances to I get you're not milking me for information?"

"You killed the only man I've ever loved," Nigel said. "I will never have him because of you. You're going away for a long time. I have nothing to live for. Couldn't we work together?"

Kyetti let out a short breath through his nose and shook his head. "You're good. I'll give you that. You had me going for a moment. Tears in those gorgeous eyes of yours. But you know what's missing in your performance?" Nigel swallowed. "Truth. If you truly lost the man you love there's a dead piece of you living in your heart. And it shows in the eyes. You can't fake it. Not when he's still alive and you have hope of going back to him as soon as you walk out the door. Look me in the eyes, Nigel. See that dead piece of me living inside. He'll know it soon enough. When he holds your broken bloody body to his chest, weeping over you. He'll know and he'll come to me. And then I will see a kindred spirit. I will see the dead eyes, the heart only beating because this world is too cruel to stop it when the rest of you dies. I will see no tears in his eyes as he looks at me and I will revel in it. He will beg. He will plead. And I will grant him nothing but your death. So, to answer your ignorant question, I got the person to tell me about your missions for sport."

Nigel leaned back in his chair faced with the darkness before him that went far deeper than any of them knew. Kyetti's dead eyes did tell a story. And that story was one of death and hate. He had failed. Gabe was still alive and there was only so much acting he could do. When faced with a master of reading people, he had failed. Then his blood ran cold as he remembered. Kyetti had called him Nigel. He hoped Kiter had only pretended to cut the audio and cameras because he suddenly needed to get out of there. Standing, he headed for the door.

"We will not meet again, Nigel Sweet. But I'm sure I'll be seeing Gabriel very soon."

Nigel swallowed hard and banged on the door. It opened and he ran out, down the hall, and toward the bathrooms. Kiter yelled his name as he ran after him, but Nigel couldn't stop. He threw open a stall door and just barely made it over the toilet when the contents of his stomach ejected themselves, with bone wracking force, out of his mouth. *Oh god, what have I done?*

Chapter Eighteen

Gabe's eyes were crossing at the mess of letters swimming in front of him as his phone dinged 2100. He was happy for the reprieve when he excused himself to call his boys.

"Daddy!" They answered with wide toothy smiles and fresh clean faces, pjs on, and hair shiny still wet from their baths.

"How are my boys?" Gabe grinned.

"Good!" Hunter said.

"When are you coming home, daddy?" Colton asked.

"What, tired of us already?" Gabe heard his dad's voice off screen.

"No, grandpa, I love it here. That's why I was asking. You let me have biscuits whenever I want," Colton loudly whispered conspiratorially as only a six-year-old could.

Gabe chuckled. "You'll have to suffer a couple more nights being spoiled by your grandparents, boys."

"Oh no!" Colton sighed then giggled as he leaned into his grandfather appearing beside them.

"You okay, daddy?" Hunter asked.

"I'm good, son, how about you? How's school?"

Gabe talked to his sons for another fifteen minutes until Colton began yawning. His dad took the phone when Hunter offered it after saying *goodnight.*

"Love you! See you soon," Gabe called as his eldest helped his youngest up the stairs to bed at their grandparents' house.

"They've been little angels," his dad said. "Well, not so little anymore."

"God, dad, where did the time go? I literally feel like it was just yesterday Colton was born. And Hunter? Jesus, he'll be a teenager in three years."

"Trust me, son, I'm looking at my thirty-five-year-old son and I swear he was in Junior Rugby League last month," his dad said.

Gabe breathed a laugh. So much had changed for him in the last month he couldn't imagine. "If you only knew."

His dad was quiet for a long moment just studying him. Gabe resisted the urge to squirm. "You know, son, I'm here if you need to talk. You couldn't say anything or do anything that would shock me, anger me, or make me love you less. You know that, right?"

"Dad, I-" Gabe took a breath, not a deep one because his chest felt heavy with fear. Would his father understand? Movement down the hall caught his eye. He looked up over the top of his phone to see Nigel and Kiter walking back. Sweet was nodding at something Kiter said and he looked so beautiful, but he was pale, and his eyes were shadowed. Still, when he locked eyes with Gabe, he smiled softly at him, and Gabe felt his lips stretch up.

No more closet for me, baby. He remembered his words the first time they kissed in the car. As if he felt Gabe's need, Nigel said something to Kiter and started down the hallway to him.

"I like whoever put that smile on your face," his dad said, and it brought Gabe back to the phone call. "Will you tell me who they are?"

Gabe blinked in surprise. His father hadn't asked who *she* was. He had said *they* gender neutral. And he felt his chest pain ease and morph into his throat as tears gathered in his eyes. Nigel had met him by then and took his hand in his, staying on the other side of the phone so his dad couldn't see him.

"Dad," he started, and it felt right. "I do have something to tell you and I hope this doesn't change anything but," he glanced up again and locked eyes with Nigel, then back at his dad on video call. "I realized on this business trip that I am in love. In love, with Nigel Sweet." He swallowed watching his dad's reaction. "And I... love him so much I can't live without him." Something clouded Nigel's eyes but Gabe tried to ignore it. "We are together. Boyfriends. I've never felt this way before for anyone. I don't classify myself as gay as I'm not attracted to any other man but maybe bi? I don't know the label."

"You don't need a label, son. You are you. And I've known you've loved him since you were eighteen. Your mother and I noticed a deeper connection between you over the last couple years that's why we've been trying to drop hints that we know and it's okay. We love you, son, and we love Nigel. He's a wonderful man and a great godfather to the boys. They don't stop talking about how, and I quote, 'amazingly awesomely cool he is'."

Nigel beamed and the glow on his face stole Gabe's breath.

"Is he there with you?" His dad asked. Gabe nodded and Nigel walked around to wave at the phone.

"Hi, Mr. Collins," he said.

"I think it's high time you call me Gerald, son, don't you?" He replied.

"No sir, I'll never be able to do that," Nigel smiled. "My mama raised me to respect the men who have earned it. And you've earned it by the bucket load sir."

Gabe's dad chuckled. "Well, it's open whenever you decide. You take care of my boy, now."

"Always, sir."

"Good," his dad looked back up at him. "I love you, Gabe. We'll talk more when you come pick up the boys. Take your time. Your mother and I love having them here."

"Thanks, Dad. Really, you have no idea how much this means to me."

"Be yourself, always. Didn't we teach you that?"

"You did."

"And that we love you no matter what?"

"Yes, sir."

"Good, then I see no point in worrying, do you?"

"No."

"All right, then. Your boys are safe, and we'll talk more later."

"Thank you, Dad."

"Bye, Mr. Collins!" Nigel called as he hung up. Nigel turned to Gabe and squeezed his hand. "How do you feel?"

Gabe took a breath. "I knew they were open and didn't have a single bigoted bone in their bodies, but sometimes it hits differently when it's your kid, ya know? I didn't realize they already knew even before I did. I don't know, it's just... a little overwhelming, if I'm honest."

"Baby," Nigel said. "If you weren't overwhelmed, I'd be worried."

"One down, now I need to tell the boys and Mum. But I doubt they'll dislike the idea," Gabe teased. "You are *amazingly awesomely cool.*"

"Yes I am, and don't you forget it, Collins," Nigel beamed.

Gabe paused, his smile still on his face but he saw how pale Nigel still was. He passed a hand over his forehead and cupped his jaw. "Are you all right? You look... worried."

"Kyetti was... intense."

"Did he say anything?"

Nigel took a breath. "It's not good. I didn't act the way I should have, and he figured it out. He threatened me." Gabe took a step closer. "Threatened you. He knew our names somehow. I'm... scared, Gabe. If anything were to happen to you or the boys because of me, I would never forgive myself."

"Hey, nothing is going to happen."

"Just promise me, you'll never go to him if something happens to me."

"What? Of course not, but nothing is going to happen to you."

"I don't know... I just don't know."

"Don't let him get into your head. That's when things get nasty."

Nigel nodded. "You're right."

"Collins, Sweet," Callum called from the doorway to the briefing room. "We need you both inside." They nodded and headed down the hall keeping each other's hand in their own as they entered the briefing room.

Chapter Nineteen

"Kyetti was less than forthcoming." Kiter was saying as they entered, and Nigel cleared his mind of everything that had just happened with Kyetti and Gabe. He needed to remain focused. How had Kyetti known his name? How did he know Gabe's? One thing was beyond question, his threats needed to be taken seriously. "It is now plainly obvious that Kyetti has someone inside the organization of MI6 who has firsthand knowledge about our missions." Kiter went on. "And about us." He clicked around on a laptop and the video, which Kiter did not cut, of Sweet's encounter with Kyetti played. Gabe gripped his hand as he watched. Once the video was over, Kiter went on. "It is very possible your lives are at risk. Boyd, could you pull the personnel files and see who has accessed them within the last week?"

"On it."

"We have an update on the PigPen Cipher and if his body

language was anything to go by, he was nervous that we got it," Callum said.

"Let's hear the update." Kiter took a seat beside Rhys as Vidar stepped up and began writing on the board holding the packet of papers the rest of the team had started decoding when he and Kiter left to speak with Kyetti.

The words were denoted by a slash mark but though it was familiar, Nigel didn't recognize the root language until Vidar wrote the word *veritas.*

"Latin?" Nigel questioned.

"Modern Latin," Boyd piped up. "The type used in Masses and songs."

"And you can read it?" Nigel stated.

Boyd nodded. "Catholic upbringing, then Catholic orphanage before state took over. I studied more to feel closer to my family when they…" he cleared his throat and looked away.

"What does it say?" Kiter questioned.

"'All things end in truth and in truth we find the end of all things'," Boyd translated.

"That's on every page of this as a header so to speak. The rest of the document we're still translating. It's a bit gibberish but we didn't expect this to be easy."

"No not at all. A code within a code possibly," Kiter agreed. Then, after a quick sigh, "Boyd, any updates on the files?"

"As far as I can see the only one to access any personnel files within this last month was Marjorie. I'll keep digging. It'll be easier if I'm onsite. Crash in the rooms downstairs?" Boyd asked.

"Of course. All right, we're all beat. You're all welcome to use the rooms downstairs again. But I know some of you are eager to get home. Let's pick this up at 1030. Thank you all for your hard work on this. Stay vigilant. Stay safe. See you tomorrow."

With that, everyone stood and headed out, apart from Boyd. Gabe offered the takeaway container he had at his desk. "Wanna eat here? Or go home?"

"Home. I need my own bed... and my hot boyfriend in it," Nigel replied.

"That sounds marvelous. I'll even feed you your curry naked," Gabe teased.

Nigel groaned and pressed his forehead against Gabe's.

"Still haven't told him, huh?" Rhys came up beside them heading to the exit at the back of the room.

"Told me what?" Gabe questioned.

"Do not reveal any of my secrets, Rhys Angus Campbell," Nigel grumbled. Rhys chuckled.

"Secrets? I like secrets," Gabe's voice betrayed his excitement.

"Food is his love language. You cooking for him in gray joggers? Yeah, I heard about that. Feed him and you'll always get lucky," Rhys revealed.

"Shhh," Nigel lightly smacked Rhys on the shoulder. "No fair."

"Ohhoho," Gabe grinned looking down at Nigel. "I love finding out secrets." His eyes sparkled with mischief.

"Get home, you two," Kiter called. "No sex in the briefing room."

"You're one to talk, Somm," Rhys replied. "I distinctly remember coming all over that table."

"I'm the boss, I can do what I please," Kiter teased.

"Ugh, good thing I didn't eat on that table like poor Vidar. He wouldn't be happy if he knew," Gabe teased.

"It's been disinfected since then. Might have to dirty it up again though," Kiter wiggled his eyebrows suggestively as he spanked Rhys' ass.

"My old back needs an actual bed, Sommerset. And you need food. Let's go home," Rhys said reaching for his boyfriend.

Once they were alone apart from Boyd in his own world doing research, Gabe pulled Nigel close and buried his nose in his neck. "Are you sniffing me?" Nigel laughed.

"You always smell so good. Like coconut, leather, and mine," Gabe answered taking another deep sniff.

"Leather is my body wash. Coconut is the lotion mama sends me from home, and as far as being yours?" He pulled back to look at him. "I've always been."

"And always will be." Gabe pressed his lips to Nigel's and sighed.

They only pulled back when Nigel's stomach growled loudly. Laughing, Nigel took Gabe's hand. "Come on," he said. "Let's go home where you can speak my love language until you can't speak any longer."

"I like the sound of this plan."

Gabe woke slowly the next morning. Taking a deep breath in, his nose was teased by soft coconut and man. His man. Opening his eyes, he couldn't help the lovesick sigh that escaped him when he saw the back of Nigel's head. Big spoon to Sweet's little spoon,

Gabe's arms were wrapped around him. His right arm tossed over his middle, his left, numb from having lost circulation sometime through the night, was in the crook of Nigel's neck, his head resting on the pillow. His right leg was sandwiched between Nigel's and his hardening morning erection was cradled by Nigel's ass.

Gabe took a deep breath in. He could smell nothing, but Nigel and he loved it. He wanted him... again. They had made love until well past one in the morning, but he couldn't get enough of him. His gasps, moans, hearing Gabe's name on his lips as he came, almost like a prayer. Damn, Gabe shifted his hips involuntarily so his aching shaft could press more firmly against Nigel's buttocks.

His man moaned softly and pushed his ass to Gabe's aching cock. "Fuck," Gabe breathed and began placing kisses on Nigel's shoulder and neck. Nigel reached and held the back of Gabe's head in place as he kissed his way up and down. Gabe's right hand spread up Nigel's stomach and chest, caressing his nipples. Nigel shuddered.

"What are you doing to me?" He questioned.

"I thought I was being obvious, I guess not," Gabe teased. He could say no more as Nigel's grip on his hair increased and Sweet turned his head around latching his lips onto Gabe's.

They both let out a needy groan as their tongues toyed with each other. Nigel turned to lie on his back as Gabe moved to hover over him. He loved the feel of his hot, hard lover beneath him. Nigel was right to warn him when he said there was nothing soft about him. He was no woman, the very insistent proof of that was trapped between them and as Gabe's hand slipped down Nigel's chest to his stomach, then lower to wrap around his shaft, he realized he never wanted another woman in his bed ever again. He wanted this. His lover, his boyfriend, his best friend. Distracted by his thoughts, he let out a surprised yelp when Nigel flipped them over and straddled Gabe's hips.

"Rule one," he looked down at him panting. "No distracting thoughts when you're in bed with me." He grinned and taking both of them in his hand, he stroked them together. "Rule two, you start something, you better finish it." Reaching for the lube they'd left on the nightstand; Nigel flipped the top open and squeezed the liquid onto his fingers. Quickly coating his hand, he took them both in one and stroked them together. Gabe gasped. He'd seen frotting in porn, but he never knew how good it would feel.

"Fuckin' hell," he gasped and arched his back like a cat. "Shit that feels good."

"There's so much I want to do to you and to this body of yours." Nigel's free hand caressed Gabe's tight stomach and fanned the muscles of his obliques. "You know how many wet dreams I had as a teenager? Even now, I dream of this body."

"Only love me for my looks, huh?" Gabe gasped out with a crooked grin.

"Not just," Nigel winked. "But damn you are hot."

Gabe stoked up Nigel's thighs still straddling his hips, the coarse black hair tickling his palms.

"You are beautiful," Gabe breathed. "Even when I thought I was straight, I always loved seeing your skin. The contrast to my own. Everything the same and yet different. I'd watch you in the dressing room. I know how creepy that sounds but just seeing you so beautiful and confident." Gabe took a breath. "I'm sorry it took me so long to realize how I feel about you."

"You never thought of anyone else like that. I'm a man. You had only ever been with women, I get it. You never have to say you're sorry for anything, my love. You came out when you wanted to. And I cannot tell you how proud I am of you."

Cupping his face, Gabe locked eyes with him. Nigel's stroking had slowed and became lazy so they both could keep a clear head while talking. But Gabe wanted to feel his man.

"Could you touch me?"

"Anywhere you want, baby. Tell me."

"Finger me. I want to feel your fingers inside me. I've never gone all the way. I'd been so tempted to get a dildo the first time, but I was too scared to."

Nigel smiled down at him softly. "If you want, we can work up to that."

"I do. I want to feel you inside me, but I'm nervous."

"And that's okay. Let's start slow. You guide me with what you're ready for. You tell me when to stop and I'll stop. Whatever you want."

"Right now, I want just your fingers. "

"Then that's what you'll get, baby."

Nigel squeezed from fresh lube and coated the fingers on his other hand. Slowly circling Gabe's entrance, he watched him. Gabe knew he was going slow for him, but he nodded quickly and Nigel slowly slipped in. The initial sting was still something Gabe didn't particularly enjoy but knowing it was Nigel made it even better. His finger was thicker than any other he'd had but it wasn't unpleasant. Nigel didn't tease, he found his prostate and Gabe gasped. The pressure was so good and when Nigel took them both in his other hand while stroking over that magical spot inside him

Gabe was lost to the sensations.

After a short time, Nigel picked up the pace. Their chests rising and falling rapidly. No more words were spoken. None were needed. They locked eyes and neither budged. Gabe felt the tell-tale heat through his body the feeling of being drawn back about to be launched heavenward. Nigel added a second finger to his hole and teased the head of his cock. Gabe let loose a cry.

Gabe's groan of pleasure was swallowed in Nigel's mouth as he leaned down and attacked his lips with his own.

His chest heaved as he gasped in breath after breath and Gabe saw the moment Nigel couldn't hold back.

"Come for me, baby," was all it took before Gabe heard Nigel cry out and felt the hot jets streak across his chest. The feel of his lover letting go triggered his own release. He clamped down on Nigel's fingers and flew. Nigel collapsed over him in a sweaty sticky panting mess and Gabe loved every second of it. Slowly, Nigel pulled his fingers out of him and Gabe felt so empty. His hole twitched nearly begging his fingers back inside him, but the sting in his arse made him pause that thought. Sweets kissed his way across his chest. He grunted when teeth closed gently over his nipple. Nigel grinned as he looked up at him.

"You okay?" Nigel said.

"What can I say? You have skills," Gabe teased.

"Oh baby, it's just the tip of the iceberg." As if stressing his point, he took Gabe's other nipple into his mouth and laved his tongue, nipping the bud with his teeth. Gabe grunted as the sensitive flesh pebbled under Nigel's expert tongue. Without warning, he popped the bud out of his mouth and swung his legs over, no longer straddling him. "Come on, make me breakfast. We need to get going."

Gabe watched languidly from the bed as Nigel stood and walked around the room leading toward the door. Gabe gave him a wolf whistle and Nigel tossed his head back laughing. Then, they both froze. Gabe's phone was ringing beside him. He swallowed as he recognized the ringtone. He didn't need to look at the name to know his soon-to-be-ex-wife was calling him. He locked eyes with Nigel standing in the doorway. He had a worried look on his face. The ringtone ended but the tension in the room remained.

"Sweets, I-"

"You should have answered it," he said.

"No," Gabe sat up and swung his legs over the edge of the bed. Standing, he hurried over to him. "I'm not going back to that, you know that, right? You're it for me."

Nigel swallowed hard, just as his phone rang again. "You should answer, it could be the boys."

"Dad would call, not her."

Nigel pulled him into a hard kiss then broke away. "Answer it. It's okay. I'll be in the shower."

With a huff, Gabe watched him walk away. Anger flowed through him. What right did Amelie have to call? All contact was to be made between their solicitors. He snatched his phone and stabbed the accept button.

"What?" He barked into the receiver.

"Gabriel?" Her voice once sexy to him with her French accent, now grated on his nerves.

"You called me, what do you think? What do you want? All communication was to go between our solicitors."

"I..."

"I need to get to work, so keep it quick. What do you want?" He demanded.

"I wanted to talk."

"Talk? So talk," he spat.

"Could you meet me? Come over for coffee?" She asked. If he were focusing on her tone, he would have heard the soft, hurting voice but he wasn't, and he didn't notice it. The only thing he heard was Nigel asking him two days ago if Amelie called wanting to make it work would he, for the boys' sake? Two days ago he wasn't sure, but at that moment, he was absolutely positive of one thing. The answer was no.

"How many times could we have talked? Hmm? How many times could you have told me you were unhappy? How many times did I try to talk to you, but you were too busy with your book club, or volunteer work, or..." a realization hit him like a ton of bricks. "My god, did you ever have book club? Were you even volunteering? Or was that the excuse you gave when you were with a bloke?"

Her silence was answer enough for him. "You missed the boys' games! Their awards ceremony! Dinners out as a family! For what?" He shouted so loudly Nigel ran out of the bathroom and hurried to him.

"I-" Amelie tried.

"No, I want none of your vague excuses. Was I so horrible as a husband that you had to disappoint our sons over and over and over again just to be satisfied?"

"Gabriel," she sighed. "I owe you and the boys so many apologies. Please, I don't want to lose the good we had."

"Good? You think it was good? Let me tell you something,

Amelie, and I want you to listen well. The best part of my life with you was my boys. That's it. I never *loved* you. I know what love is now, and I never had it for you."

"What?" She demanded and it was like a switch had been flipped like the day she had attached him. She screamed at him. "You have someone else? Already? Who is the little *pute*, huh? We're still married, or have you forgotten? You cheated on me too? Was it some sort of payback? Who is she?"

"He is none of your business." That shut her up. "Any further communication is to be strictly between our solicitors. Do not call or text me or the boys. Oh, and by the way, I know about you hitting Hunter. And all I have to say is thank god I have all the evidence I need. You will never see the boys again. Now, kindly fuck off." He angrily hung up his phone. He was shaking. "Damn her, damn her straight to hell," he shouted.

"Hey hey, easy baby," Nigel tried to soothe.

"Sweets, I'm too angry right now, please. I'm way too angry. I don't want to hurt you."

"Breathe, Gabe, breathe, baby."

He turned his wild eyes to him but instead of backing up as lesser men would, Nigel slipped his arms around Gabe and held on. Gabe couldn't wrap his arms around Sweets. He was too full of vile hate from his ex-wife. He didn't want to contaminate Nigel's goodness and purity.

"It's all right. Everything is all right. I love you. She is out of your life and out of Hunter's and Colton's lives. Come back to me, baby. Be with me. You're safe here in my arms. I love you, Gabe Collins, don't ever forget that."

With that, Gabe broke on an angry sob and clutched Nigel

to him. He screamed into his lover's neck and tears flowed. He mourned not the loss of his wife, but the loss of all the years he had wasted on her when he could have had the man in his arms, a good man, the best friend he ever could have hoped for, if only he had been brave enough to admit his feelings were never fully platonic. He wept because in thinking that, did he wish his sons away? He was a tangled-up mess of knots like the ones at a shipyard museum he had visited as a kid. He loved his boys, and he loved Nigel. But at that moment, he needed to see his boys. Even just long enough to embrace them, feel their love surround him, revel in their sweetness. Maybe that was selfish, but he didn't care. Through his sniffles and tight chest, he pulled back and looked at Nigel. His best friend's face was open and kind. Loving. He rested his forehead against Nigel's. "I need to see my boys."

"All right," Sweets answered. "Go, I'll cover for you. It's 0825 now, if you head up now, you'll get there by 0930. Try to be back by 1130 though or Kiter might have my arse."

Gabe growled and squeezed said arse "It's mine."

Nigel giggled and shook his head. "Get dressed. I'll fry up some eggs. Eat before you hit the road."

"I love you," Gabe called after him as he slipped away.

Throwing a kiss over his shoulder, Nigel sauntered to the kitchen while Gabe jumped into the shower, dressed, and ate quickly.

Chapter Twenty

His boys' love was the healing balm he needed and to see his parents so easily accepting of his new relationship with Nigel was a weight lifted off his shoulders. He left their house an hour after he had arrived, rejuvenated, and with a promise he would bring Nigel back with him when he came to pick up the boys the next day. His mother made him promise to tell Nigel she would make him his favorite dessert as incentive. Waving and blowing kisses to his family as he pulled down the drive, he settled into his seat for the long drive back to HQ. The closer he got, the happier he became. His father told him Amelie was in violation of the terms set forth by the divorce proceedings and he promised to contact her solicitor and the barristers who would try the case if it went to trial. They both fully expected it to end up in court. Amelie wasn't going to go away silently.

An alert pinged on his phone's GPS, and he listened to the

AI voice tell him of a quicker route. To save three hours, he needed to take the next exit.

"Three hours?" He questioned. "Might as well. Sweets'll kill me if I'm late." He chuckled.

The new route took him down a side street and as he looked across the annex road to see the reason for the delay, the flashing lights of both police and fire brigade greeted him. A mangled car flipped on its roof looked totaled on the motorway. From his quick glance and years of experience with similar situations, it looked near fatal if not completely. Cars were backed up as far as he could see since the motorway was shut down. Debris of the car was scattered in both lanes.

"Poor bugger," he muttered shaking his head.

The rest of the thirty-minute drive was uneventful and as he pulled into his spot, he glanced to his right. Sweet's, Vidar's, and Rhys' cars weren't in their space. Only Kiter's BMW sat in the garage. He hurried to the door and badged in. On his way up the elevator, he pulled out his phone only realizing he'd had it on DO NOT DISTURB as he drove.

Switching it off and before his notifications had time to populate, he glanced up and saw Kiter leaning against the briefing room door, waiting for him.

"Hey boss, sorry I'm late. Did Sweets explain everything?" He asked. Kiter just stared at him and took a deep breath. Confused, and desperately trying to ignore the knots forming in his gut, he spoke again. "What's up? Everything all right? Where is everyone?"

"Gabe," Kiter sighed. "They're at hospital."

"Hospital? Why? Did something happen? Is someone

hurt?"

"Gabe." Kiter placed his hands on Gabe's shoulders and stared deeply into his eyes. "It's Nigel."

"Nigel? What?"

"There was a car accident on A3204."

"What?" Gabe couldn't get his breath. Ears ringing, tongue thick, grey specks filled his vision.

"There was an accident on the A3204. He was driving in and according to witnesses, he swerved, and the car went airborne when it hit the curb. It flipped and landed on the roof. He is alive according to the last report but, it's not good. Rhys said the doctor's prognosis isn't good. I stayed here to wait for you and call his parents. We're flying them in."

"Boss," Gabe was shaking violently, and his legs gave out. He had seen the wreckage. He knew the injuries. "Is he... is... he..." he couldn't bring himself to say the words. Kiter crouching down to be eye level with him.

"He's alive right now. I'm not going to sugar coat it, Gabe. I don't know if he's going to make it."

Gabe let out a sob and gripped Kiter's lapels. "He has to. He has to."

Kiter's lips were pressed together in a thin line. "Come on, let's go to hospital. He's still in surgery. But you can be there... just in case."

Gabe couldn't move. His body weak. He couldn't see Kiter through the grey mist circling before his eyes. Kiter helped him stand and kept his arms around him as they got to the elevator, then the car.

The closer they got to the hospital, the more nervous

energy escaped Gabe. He needed to see him. He needed to hear his voice. Kiter slid the car into the first open parking spot and threw it into park. Gabe was out the door before the car stopped rocking. They nearly ran into the emergency doors.

"Somm," they heard Rhys call to them.

Turning to see Rhys, Callum, Vidar, and Boyd in the waiting room, they hurried toward them.

"Any news?" Gabe demanded choosing to ignore the paleness of Rhys' face and the stoic looks others were giving him.

Rhys shook his head. "Not for some time. It's not good, Gabe."

"Did you see him?"

"No, we got the call after he was taken to surgery. Reception has given us updates but can't divulge too much."

"That's unacceptable." Gabe stalked over to the glass partition and stared until the man seated at the desk looked up. "I need an update on Nigel Sweet."

"Are you family?" The man asked.

"I'm his boyfriend," Gabe said.

The man nodded. "Let me see what I can find out."

Gabe tapped his fingers against his thigh. He hated waiting. He needed to know if Nigel... he swallowed. He had to be okay. The man clicked around on the computer, then nodded.

"He's still in surgery. But I will be sure to get you back there when he's in his room."

"Can you tell me anything?" Gabe demanded.

"I'm sorry. I'm at the mercy of updates to the system. Doctors don't update while they're in theater. But no news right now is good news."

Gabe gave a harsh sigh and stalked back to the team.

"They're in the air, should land around midnight," Kiter was saying when Gabe walked up. They all turned to him. "Did they tell you anything?"

"No," Gabe grunted. "I need to see him. I need to know. I need-" his chest hurt, and he couldn't catch his breath again.

Rhys and Vidar grabbed his arms and guided him to one of the chairs before his knees gave out.

"I need to hear his voice," he felt the tears on his cheeks and Boyd slipped his hand into his and squeezed. He looked over and Boyd tried to have an encouraging smile on his face, but it fell flat.

"Do you have any voicemails or video?" Boyd offered. "It's not the same, I know. But when my grandpa died, I kept his last voicemail until... well, you weren't allowed to have a phone at the orphanage. But it helped me for a time."

Gabe squeezed Boyd's hand then dropped it and grabbed his phone. He hadn't checked it since he'd taken it off DO NOT DISTURB. He saw the texts and calls from the men standing near him but there was one from Nigel. His hand shook so badly he could barely click play. He raised the phone to his ear.

"Hey baby," he heard Nigel's voice and he sobbed. What if that was the last time he heard him? *"I'm heading into HQ. Be safe. Let those amazing boys fill you with the love they give so freely. I love you and oh shit!"* Gabe's grip on his phone increased. *"Oh my god, they're shooting at me!"* Gabe heard the pinging and glass breaking. *"Shit! I'm hit! Fuck! Oh my god... Gabe, I love you."* Then the scariest sound Gabe had ever heard, resounded in his ear. The horrifying sound of Nigel's car flipping and crashing on its roof.

No, that was the second most horrifying sound. The number one spot was filled with the next sound. Nigel's wet, labored breathing. Gabe's body tingled as his blood pressure skyrocketed. There was silence for a short moment then Gabe heard a new voice over the phone.

"This is what happens to men who meddle. You were warned. Kyetti says hello."

Nigel grunted and his next word shook Gabe to the core. *"S-s-s-sa-Sasha?"*

There was the sound of a gunshot and cursing in Russian, then the voicemail ended.

Gabe sat there, the phone still at his ear. His ears ringing.

"Gabe?" He looked up suddenly almost scared out of his trance. "What's going on?" Rhys asked.

His lips tingling, he licked them and looked up at the others around him. "Sasha. It was Sasha."

"What? What was?" Boyd questioned.

Swallowing the bile in his mouth, Gabe played the voicemail and put it on speaker. Everyone listened and had visible reactions to the sound of the accident. But when they heard Nigel name the man, the shock gave way to anger.

Kiter grabbed his phone and dialed. "Marjorie, gather everything you have on Oleksandr Demidov and meet me at the hospital. Bring the big van. We need to set up a mobile headquarters." He hung up, anger barely contained.

"Somm, don't do anything stupid," Rhys placed his hand on his boyfriend's arm.

He shook his head. "Calculating," he answered and dialed another number. "Sash, hey mate, how are you?" His voice was carefree as he spoke. "Oh yeah? Good, good yeah. One of my agents was in a car accident but good... oh yeah, he's fine actually. He's still at hospital but he's up and talking... hm?... oh no, he doesn't remember anything that happened, right now. He just mentioned you were there so I wanted to thank you. I figured you called emergency services for him... well, I appreciate it. Hey, since you're in town, Leo and I would love to have you over for dinner tonight... oh, damn well maybe tomorrow night then? You can't leave without tasting Leo's lasagna. Great! I'll send you our address. Looking forward to seeing you." His smile wiped off his face as soon as he lowered the phone.

"What did you tell him that for?" Boyd asked.

"He's a spy. He'll know what I'm doing, so I had to try a different approach. Put him off guard and on guard at the same time. If he thinks Nigel knows anything, he'll come after him. I want him transferred to a secure facility in the basement of MI6 and we'll put a decoy in the bed. We'll stake it out. Capture him in the act. One down."

"You don't think he's the one behind Hes and Dare's deaths do you?" Boyd had a disgusted look on his face. "Oh my god, I slept with him. I let him touch me. Do things to me. I think I'm going to be sick."

"You're not the only one," Kiter stated. "He's involved but I don't think he was behind their deaths. He was on mission when they died. We have someone else to find but he's obviously working with them."

Boyd looked green and he wrapped his arms around his middle. Vidar placed a hand on his shoulder.

"Now, we're going to need to-"

"Family for Nigel Sweet?" A doctor entered the room and Gabe's stomach dropped. He couldn't speak. The woman asking for him had the power to either shatter him or patch him together.

Kiter raised his hand, and she walked over. Gabe wasn't sure his legs would cooperate, but he was able to stand, leaning heavily on Rhys' arm.

"Family for Nigel Sweet?" the doctor asked again, closer that time. She was looking at them expectantly.

"Yes," Gabe cleared his throat. "Yes, sorry. I'm his boyfriend."

"His parents are on their way," Kiter explained. "We work together."

"Of course, well, Mister..." she looked at Gabe.

"Collins," he answered out of habit.

"Mr. Collins, your boyfriend suffered major trauma. He's alive but we won't know the extent of his injuries until he wakes up."

Gabe swallowed wanting to know, but also not wanting to know.

"He had a compound fracture to his left leg and crushed the right. His clavicle was dislocated, and he had a bullet wound in his right shoulder. His lower spine was also impacted. Now, I've done all I can, but it might impact his ability to walk. As for internal organs, he had a lacerated spleen and a punctured lung. Brain function seems to be normal, but we are monitoring for brain swelling. He has a very long road to recovery."

Gabe nodded slowly, his brain not fully comprehending everything she said. "Can I see him?"

"Yes, I'll take you back there."

"Can he be moved?" Kiter asked.

"To where, precisely?" Her tone showed her disapproval.

"A more secured and personalized facility," Kiter said.

"I would highly recommend Mr. Sweet stay exactly where he is."

"That's not possible, I'm afraid. As soon as he is able to be moved, he will need to be," Kiter said.

"Without a court order, I refuse to allow it."

"You'll have it on your desk in an hour," Kiter promised and turned away tapping on his phone.

"Please, can I see him?" Gabe begged the doctor.

She huffed once and looked at him. "He's very fragile right now, Mr. Collins. You must understand he suffered major injuries and cannot be moved."

"I understand. Please, I just need him protected and I need to see him."

She took a breath and nodded. "Follow me." He followed her down the sterile hallway and around a couple corners to a room. "Prepare yourself," she said, hand on the doorknob.

He swallowed hard and nodded. She opened the door and his heart nearly stopped. Sweets was lying prone on his back. Clad in a hospital gown with tubes coming out of his mouth, an IV in his hand, and oxygen under his nose. His legs were in casts, his upper body wrapped to keep him still and his neck was in a brace. His face was scratched and bruised. His eyes were closed and the only proof he was alive was the constant beeping from one of the machines around him.

"Sweets," he sobbed. "Baby." He rushed to his side.

"Talk to him," the doctor said, still at the door. "He can hear you." She gave a tight smile and left the room.

He took Nigel's hand. His body felt light, almost floating, like he was in a dream, instead of living a nightmare. He stared at his lover for the longest time, until he grabbed the chair behind him and pulled it closer to the bed. Slowly he leaned down to kiss him. "I'm here, baby. I love you and we're going to get the man who did this to you."

He sat in the chair and covered Sweet's hand with his and stared. Remembering all the times they had together and hoping for all the times in the future, he stayed and stared and willed his best friend back to him.

His body felt numb. And what he could feel was pain. Massive pain.

"...remember that it was fun." A voice penetrated the haze of his mind. He knew that voice.

Gabe.

The voice sighed. "Baby, please wake up. I need you, please."

I'm trying. I'm trying.

Blackness faded in and he slept blissfully pain free.

"...wakes, call me immediately. I'll need to verify he has feeling..."

Fade.

"...stayed all night at hospital but Sasha didn't show."

Sasha? I know something about him. Something... what do I know?

Fade.

"...time, it'll happen. Nigel is strong." That voice. He knew that voice.

"We're just so glad they could fly us here directly, love. And we're so happy you two are together now." *Mama...*

"He means everything to me, Mrs. Sweet. I love him so much."

"Thank you, dear."

"He'll be fine. He's been through worse." *Papa,* that was his father.

"I just need him to wake up. I need to hear his voice." *Gabe...*

"He will."

I'm trying, baby. I'm here. I love you.

Fade.

Chapter
Twenty-One

Gabe paced the small room waiting. He hoped Nigel would understand why he was breaking his promise. When Sasha didn't show at the hospital as they expected to check if Nigel was alive or not, Kiter and Gabe talked. They needed to play to Kyetti's arrogance. So there he waited for the monster who ordered the hit on Nigel, to walk through the door. He was glad Kiter gave him carte blanche because he was certain he wanted to kill him.

The door opened. "You son of a bitch!" He shouted as soon as he saw him. He raced over and grabbed his shirt, slamming him against the two-way mirror.

Kyetti gave an evil smile. "Gabriel, I presume. Oh gracious, was that two days ago?" He pouted mockingly. "I'm sorry for your loss."

"Bastard!" Gabe couldn't stop it, he punched him. Hard.

Kyetti spat out some blood and a tooth. Then, locked eyes

with Gabe, searching. "Ah," he breathed softly. "There it is."

"There what is?" Gabe demanded through clenched teeth, centimeters from Kyetti's face.

"A kindred spirit."

In disgust, Gabe let Kyetti go and rammed him against the wall behind them. "I am nothing like you."

"You will be. When the pain morphs to anger."

"I'm already angry."

"Good, then the anger turns into survival. Then, you and I will be the same."

"What is your fascination with me? With Nigel?" Gabe demanded. "What did we ever do to you that you had to... do that to him?" His voice cracked and Kyetti's mouth quirked up.

"I am not a man who is easily defeated. I evened the playing field. Surely you must understand that."

Gabe stared at him for a long moment, then shook his head in disbelief. "You're a psychopath."

"Maybe but tell me. Do you honestly know who I am?"

"You're a monster."

"No, that's *what* I am. Do you know *who* I am?"

"What are you talking about?"

"Mm, this is why I much preferred talking to your lover. He was so much more intelligent than you. I'll use small words."

Gabe slammed Kyetti against the mirror again and Kyetti grinned. "I'll be sure to say hello to your sons when I meet them at the funeral. I hear Hunter is an excellent Winger, even at ten."

Gabe felt his face pale as his blood pressure and heartbeat jumped. Then, he remembered the conversation he had with Sasha when they had left the bunker for a smoke almost a week ago. But he needed more. Resisting the urge to look into the mirror where he knew Kiter was standing, he tightened his grip on Kyetti.

"How do you know so much about us?"

"I can't tell you all my secrets. But tell me, have you figured it out? Nigel would have. He was definitely the beauty and the brains while you're clearly merely the brawn. I killed the wrong man, didn't I? Pity."

Gabe threw his fist against Kyetti's chin and brought him closer. "Who are you? How do you know all this?!" Spittle jumped from Gabe's mouth to Kyetti's face.

"You tell me," Kyetti stated, unfazed by his outburst. "This goes so much deeper than any of you realized. You think a little roughing up will get me to talk? Does he?" He turned his head slightly toward the mirror then back at Gabe. "I was tortured for my country by my country. Do you honestly think *you* stand a chance at breaking me?"

"Is Sasha working for you?"

His lips turned up revealing his bloody teeth from where Gabe's punches had landed. "Not as dumb as you look."

"So help me, I will kill you if I have to."

"Dead men tell no tales, or so I'm told."

"I don't need you. I'll figure it out without you."

"No, you won't," Kyetti stated. "You think your little rag tag group of misfits will be able to solve this? You need to ask yourself one question, Gabriel."

"What's that?"

"Who am I? If I'm just a broker, then there's two sides to every transaction." Kyetti leaned in and whispered. "Who's on the other side?"

"That's quite enough." A voice said as the door opened. "Agent Collins, unhand my client."

"Your client?" Gabe stepped back and looked at the man.

"You'll have to forgive him. Not very bright, this one," Kyetti said.

"Donovan Stuart," the man handed Gabe his card. Gabe read and then looked up sharply at the mirror then turned to the solicitor.

"Immigration and Asylum?" Gabe demanded.

"That's right, I've been retained to assist Major Kyetti with asylum. He's not to be treated like a common criminal. He's a refugee from a dangerous tyrannical government and he will be treated with the dignity owed him."

"He's a monster," Gabe spat.

"He is an asset to England, and I would appreciate it if you would refrain from using such bigoted language. We do not know his story." The solicitor set his briefcase down on the table. "Now, I would like a word with my client alone."

"Who retained you?"

"That's none of your business. And is protected by the attorney/client privilege."

"Bullshit. This man is a war criminal. He has no rights."

"I have been very nice up until this moment, Agent Collins. But if you refuse to leave the room so I may speak with him, I will be filing a writ for his immediate release from MI6's custody due to my concerns of his wellbeing. And I understand you have a pending divorce trial? Do not make me have a word with that judge. It would be a disgrace for those boys to have to live with their mother."

Gabe stared at him, his breathing picked up and his body tingled. His fight or flight was kicking in and he wanted a fight. Oh, how much he wanted a fight. But two knocks on the mirror stopped him.

The solicitor looked toward the mirror, then back at him, his mask of indifference never slipping. "Sounds like your handler wants you, guard dog. Woof woof."

Gabe straightened to his full height, a good half a foot taller than the solicitor, sucked his teeth, and walked to the door.

"I look forward to seeing you again, Agent Collins," Kyetti tossed over his shoulder as Gabe opened the door.

"As do I," Gabe answered, an icy tone to his voice. He opened the door and walked down the hall to where Kiter waited. "What the hell?"

Kiter shook his head. "I don't know. But we're going to need to find out."

"Dad... let's go talk to my dad. He knows everyone. He'll know of that beady-eyed bastard."

"Good idea." Gabe and Kiter walked down the hall to the elevators. His mind constantly churning how Kyetti knew so much. Because of Sasha, clearly, but why? And what was his end game?

Chapter Twenty-Two

Nigel opened his eyes and took in the ceiling of an unfamiliar room. He was lying on his back, his body hurt. He wasn't in the hospital, but he heard the beeping of machines as if he was. He tried to move his head, but his neck was stationary and for a brief moment he panicked until he felt the brace. He tried to move his hand and only his fingers wiggled. His upper chest was in a cast. What had happened to him? Why couldn't he remember?

In the quiet, apart from the beeping of the machine, he heard a soft snore beside him. He moved his eyes to look over and saw Gabe sitting beside his bed, asleep in a chair. He took a breath and opened his mouth.

"Gaaah," he tried to say Gabe's name, but his voice didn't work almost as if he hadn't used it in a while, and his throat was so dry.

But it was enough. Gabe jerked awake, looked at him, his

eyes widening and his mouth agape. "Baby?" He jumped up and tried to cover the short distance between them too quickly, nearly stumbling. "Baby!" He gasped when he made it to the hospital bed. "Oh my god! You're awake!" He sobbed.

The next twenty minutes was a series of tests by a doctor Nigel had never seen before. Followed by a reunion with his parents, Gabe's parents and boys, and the team. His mother kissed him all over his face while thanking god for his mercies. His father held his hand, eyes suspiciously wet. Gabe's parents stood beside the bed, happy smiles on their faces. Hunter and Colton wanted to climb up to sit on the bed, but Gabe held them back. The team all looked relieved.

"Thank god," Boyd said. "You have no idea how this guy was while you were out. Grumpy grump, I tell you."

Nigel grinned and reached his hand for Gabe who immediately grasped it. "Not sure I remember anything."

"That's okay." Kiter said. "We have the voicemail."

"Voicemail?" Nigel questioned.

"Before the crash," Gabe explained. "You had called me and were leaving me a voicemail when..."

Nigel's eyebrows furrowed. "I don't remember that."

"It's okay, the doctor said it would be completely normal. Your memory may never fully return for that traumatic situation. And maybe that's a good thing," Kiter explained.

"Yeah maybe, but there was something. Something I needed to tell you about." He tried to concentrate but couldn't. "It's like a dream. It's there, but I just can't grab it."

"We'll talk, we have some updates." Kiter's voice was cryptic.

"Could I have a moment alone with Gabe?" Nigel asked.

"Of course," his father said and helped bustle everyone out of the room.

Once they were alone, Gabe sat down on the hospital bed near Nigel's hips and kept his hand in his.

"I'm glad I still have feeling in my legs," Nigel said. "I was worried for a moment when I couldn't move my neck."

"You can't overdo it just because the doctor took the brace off."

"I won't," he promised. "And I already have a mother, thank you very much." He teased with a wink. Gabe breathed a chuckle and looked down before lifting his gaze again. "Thank you for staying with me."

"My god there's nowhere else I would be, baby," Gabe leaned down and kissed him.

Finally, Nigel thought. He had wanted to feel Gabe's lips on his since he woke. Gabe was gentle, didn't rush, and it was the sweetest kiss. When Gabe finally pulled away, he pressed his forehead to Nigel's and breathed shakily.

"What's wrong?" Nigel asked. Gabe shook his head. "Baby, talk to me. What's wrong?"

"I just-" he swallowed audibly and turned away. Nigel lifted his good arm and reached for him. Gabe leaned in so he didn't have far to move. "It's just... if I hadn't gone to see the boys and hadn't left you alone, this might not have happened."

"Don't do that to yourself," Nigel said. "I chose to drive in. I knew Kyetti's warning, and I didn't heed it." Gabe's face darkened. "What?"

"I went to go see him."

"You what? I told you-"

"I know," Gabe sighed harshly. "But Sasha didn't take the bait and we needed to do something. Kiter and I talked and the best thing was to play to his ego. It worked... sort of."

"What do you mean? What were you thinking? That man is evil."

"It's fine. I hoped you would understand. I had to do it. For the team."

Nigel heaved a sigh. His head throbbed, and he closed his eyes against the dizziness that washed over him.

"Sweets?" Gabe asked.

Nigel opened his eyes and focused on Gabe's face. The world still spun but when he focused on the gold in Gabe's eyes, it helped.

"I'm sorry," Nigel said. "I just didn't want you anywhere near that monster."

"I understand, and I didn't want to break my promise to you, but I had to see if I could break him."

"And?"

"Not all the way. Some info though. I know Kiter's eager to get you up to speed."

Nigel nodded and took a deep breath. "Could I have some water?"

Gabe reached for the cup and helped him sip it. That small exertion drained him, and he fell back to the bed which was angled so he sat up. He stared at Gabe for the longest time before he cupped his face. "I don't remember much apart from the fear of never seeing you again."

"I love you so much," Gabe said softly. "I cannot imagine

going through life without you and when I heard about the accident, I..." he swallowed. "I never want to feel that again. We go, we go together, understood?"

"Yes, sir," Nigel winked. "I could never lose you. But hey, you got me forever, Collins, you better realize that."

"Forever is what I want with you." Gabe rested his forehead against Nigel's once more and their eyes locked. "Marry me?"

Nigel's breath caught. How many times had he wanted to hear those words? He'd lost count. And to have gone through hell and back to know Gabe loved him, truly loved him as much as he loved Gabe, was heady. If he was honest with himself, he was never secure in his relationship with Gabe until that moment. He was certain he'd get tired of him or want to be with a woman or realize being gay or bi, however he identified, was too much for him and he would leave. But hearing him say those words, ask that question, solidified his place beside him.

"I want nothing more," he said. "Yes, Gabriel Collins, I will marry you whenever and wherever you want."

Cheering from across the room drew their attention and they glanced over to see their families and friends standing in the doorway cheering. Their mothers had happy tears in their eyes and their dads whooped as the CCBoys clapped and cheered. Hunter and Colton ran in and threw their arms around Gabe.

"Does this mean we'll be staying with Uncle Nigel?" Colton asked.

"Forever, little man," Nigel said. Gabe picked his youngest son up and Hunter hugged Nigel gently.

"I really wanted this," Hunter cried. "I wanted you to be

with us always. I wanted you as my second dad. I love you, Uncle Nigel."

Nigel's throat unexpectedly grew tight as he cupped Hunter's face. "I love you too, Hunter. You're such an amazing young man and I will always be here for you."

"Can... can I call you Papa?" Hunter asked.

The tears that threatened fell and Nigel tugged him close. "You can call me anything you want. But I would be honored to have that name."

Hunter clutched him close, and Nigel looked up at Gabe, happy tears filling his eyes. When the boys had their fill of hugs, Nigel's and Gabe's parents rushed in. Kisses and more hugs and their mothers embraced like the old friends they were.

"We have a wedding to plan," Nigel's mother said to Gabe's.

"Ooh, on the beach?" Gabe's mother offered.

"That would be wonderful!"

"Ladies, it's their wedding," Nigel's dad said gently.

"Thank you, Papa," Nigel replied then glanced at Gabe. "Though..."

"Beach? I mean," Gabe grinned. "Yes, please."

"There's a particular palm tree I'd like to be under when I pledge my life and love to you."

Gabe grinned. "I think I remember that palm tree."

"We're going to make the wedding perfect!" Boyd's bouncy voice came next. "Ladies, I have just the thing. It's going to be amazing!"

"Boyd, it's going to be small," Gabe cautioned.

"It's the first Charing Cross Boys wedding! It can't be

small! Not with me here. Don't worry about a thing. You just tell me your venue of choice and the date, and I'll hack the system to ensure it's yours, might get you a discount while I'm at it."

"Darling," Gabe's mother said. "You might be my favorite person."

Boyd beamed. "Just realize boys, I would do the same for you all." He turned to Rhys. "So when is the big day for you? Or are you going to be one of those boring couples who stay boyfriends and never get married?"

Rhys and Kiter exchanged a look and the corner of their lips tipped up.

"Pretty sure that ship already sailed," Gabe teased.

Rhys snapped his eyes to him. "How did you..."

"Oh please," Nigel and Callum said at the same time.

Boyd's jaw dropped comically. "You got married without telling me? Without telling us?"

"Yep," Kiter answered wrapping his arm around Rhys' waist. "Sorry."

"You're gonna be! Who was your best man if not for me?" Boyd demanded.

"My brother," Kiter said.

"And mine," Rhys answered.

"When?" Boyd asked.

"Just after Vidar came onboard," Kiter explained. "That morning we had the late meeting. Before we left on mission. Yeah, we were at the courthouse."

"Your wedding day dinner was pizza?" Boyd questioned.

"Aye, and it was good, just not as good as dessert." Rhys winked at Kiter.

Boyd's brow furrowed. "We didn't have dessert."

"Oh my god, Boyd," Gabe burst out laughing.

He looked over at Gabe, then realization dawned, and his face lit up. "Oh!" He turned to eye them. "Ooh... I bet." He grinned.

"I guess we can wear these now," Kiter said as they took out their wedding rings from their pockets, turned toward each other, and slipped them on the other's finger. Kiter pulled Rhys into a kiss.

After a few minutes of congratulations to both couples, talk about weddings, venues, and receptions, Kiter looked at Gabe, and Nigel saw the seriousness of the situation. Whatever was going on, they needed to talk. Gabe nodded and Kiter got everyone's attention with a soft clearing of his throat.

"We appreciate all of the well wishes," he said. "But we do have to bring Nigel up to speed and since the doctor wanted him to rest, we need to do so quickly. If you all wouldn't mind giving us the room for thirty minutes?"

"Oh! Of course," Nigel's mother said. "I need to check on the pork shoulder and get the Turn Cornmeal in the oven."

Nigel's stomach let out a loud growl and everyone turned to look and he chuckled. "Sorry."

"Darlin' you haven't eaten. You need to get more meat on those bones," his mother said. "I'll see if there's some stew left. These boys eat like there's no tomorrow. Especially that one." She pointed at Boyd.

"Because it's so good!" He justified.

"I love your mum's cooking," Vidar said.

"Same," everyone in the room replied.

Nigel grinned and winked at his mama. "Yeah, she is pretty

amazing." She blew her son a kiss.

"All right, my boys," Gabe's dad said to Hunter and Colton. "Let's get out of here. How about a dip in the pool?"

"Oh yes!" They both said and ran out of the room.

Nigel's mum smiled after them. "More grandbabies to spoil, Vernon. We are so blessed."

"We are, Sweetheart," Nigel's dad said and wrapped his arm around her waist. "We'll leave you boys." With a wink, they left the room.

"All right, Team," Kiter called everyone's attention once the door shut, and they were alone. "Nigel, we are beyond happy to see you are still with us." Nigel gave a soft "thank you" and Kiter went on. "We all heard the voicemail and we all hope to have matter settled."

"I'm sorry," Nigel spoke up. "I don't remember. What happened?"

Gabe leaned in and, instead of playing the voicemail and possibly triggering a PTSD episode, explained, "The accident was caught on audio. We heard Sasha's voice. We think he's working with Kyetti."

"Boyd confirmed the only visitors besides us to Kyetti was Sasha and there are several calls from Kyetti to a burner phone we believe is linked to Sasha. The reason you're here and not in hospital is because we tried to trick Sasha into thinking you were awake and trap him when or if he came to finish the job. We had Callum in your assigned room all night, but he never showed. He's dumped his burner phones and gone silent. Boyd found one of his aliases buying a plane ticket to Albania but it was too late the plane had already landed at its destination. Sasha is in the wind. We also have some... difficult news to share."

Nigel glanced over at Gabe who wouldn't look him in the eye and squirmed in his seat.

"What?"

"Yesterday, Kyetti's solicitor, who, according to Gabe's father, is ruthless and plays whatever side he needs to, was able to get him released on refugee status. He has since disappeared, and the solicitor's body was found floating in the Thames."

Nigel's heart sped up, as did the machine's beeping monitoring him. Gabe took his hand and tried to calm him. "Do we have any indication as to where he is?" Nigel asked.

"The only thing was Boyd was able to track a wire from MI6 to the solicitor's account," Rhys said.

"Well, whose name was on the wire?" Nigel questioned.

Kiter took a breath. "Marjorie's."

"What?" Nigel demanded. "No."

"Boss, there's no way," Callum replied.

"Come on," Gabe said. "It's Marjorie for god's sake."

"I agree, she wouldn't do this," Vidar finished.

"Wouldn't she? How do we know?" Rhys questioned.

"I'm the only one who knows her the best and I know next to nothing about her," Kiter explained.

"Well, now's your chance, boss." Her voice came from the doorway.

"Rhys, detain her," Kiter ordered.

Rhys stood and moved toward her. She held up a hand, the other holding a file. "I'm not going to run, and I'm unarmed. If you're going to accuse me of something, at least allow me to rebuttal," she stated.

Rhys looked at Kiter who took a deep breath but eventually nodded. Staying close behind her, Rhys followed her to his vacated seat. He stood behind the chair as she sat.

Marjorie took a deep breath and began. "My late wife was a field operative. She and I had to keep our relationship a secret because I was technically her handler, and we were in a department that was... less than friendly to gay or lesbian couples. She was sent on a mission to Russia to infiltrate, through a friendly, the FSB to find a leak that shared our agents' information and blew their covers, causing over a dozen to be killed. She was in the process of transferring the information to me when she was interrupted and..." she trailed off, her eyes misting and voice tightening. Boyd reached over and took her hand.

"Sorry," she cleared her throat and looked up. "I never saw who killed her, but the bastard shot her in the back. When I heard the voicemail, I recognized the voice. He said the same thing to Hannah. *This is what happens to those who meddle.*" She looked down as a tear slipped down her cheek. "No one knew she was there, except the friendly. Her cover was perfect and so intact that when her body was found by The FSB, they treated her as one of their own and launched an investigation into her murder. They never got anywhere, but I made it my mission to avenge her. I have since suspected someone in MI6 was ordering the agent to take out our own agents who get too close to discovering them. They've been playing both sides and murdering our agents and civilians. But I have no proof.

"When we lost Darius and Hesler," she went on. "I was certain the same person tipped off the Rentai Cartel. It just screamed *inside job.* I went to Lester, and he referred me to his boss but they refused to see me. Why, I don't know. Someone knows I'm poking around. Someone framed me with that wire payment."

"Do you know who?" Kiter questioned.

"Boyd-"

"What?" Boyd demanded, wide eyed. "No, I wouldn't. I-"

Vidar leaned closer to him; protection mode activated. "You said you have no proof. Don't just be throwing accusations out."

"I'm not," she answered.

"I didn't!" Boyd cried.

"If you would let me finish," she replied, "Boyd is the only one who can help me find the proof I need. I need him to break into a vault."

"Oh," Boyd breathed and leaned back into his chair. "That I can do."

"What vault?" Kiter questioned.

Marjorie locked eyes with him. "FCEE290717."

Kiter held her gaze for a long moment. Silence filling the room. Finally, he took a deep breath and bit his lower lip in concentration. Boyd looked from Marjorie to Kiter. "FCEE? What does that mean?"

"Marjorie, do you seriously believe someone in our government is behind those attacks?" Kiter asked.

"Yes, I do," she answered.

"What attacks?" Gabe asked.

"On 19 July 2017, there were attacks on London Bridge. The altercation with the suspect and one of our agents prevented the bomb from going off killing dozens but ended with the agent shooting the suspect off the bridge into the Thames. The suspect's body never washed ashore and was never found. It was suggested that the body washed out to sea. But as of six months ago there was no sign of him until intel surfaced that he was selling top secret information to al-Qaeda and Russian FSB including nuclear launch sequencing and self-destruct."

"Wait," Boyd said, tone clearly catching something. "Petra, our first case? Hassan Petra?"

"Exactly," Kiter agreed.

"Well, all right. He's dead, so he's of no use. Maybe we can talk to the agent who shot him? Who was the agent?" Gabe asked.

"Me," Callum spoke up. "I shot Petra."

"Ehum, sorry, for those of us who are new?" Vidar asked.

"Our first case, we lost two agents going after Petra, an expat. The Rentai Cartel had gotten there first and was waiting for us," Boyd explained then turned to Marjorie. "So you're saying, in that file, they might have information on who Petra, Sasha, even Kyetti are working for?"

"Doubtful," Kiter said. "It would be too damning. But they might have something we could tie back to the person when found. Some evidence connecting Sasha, Petra, and Kyetti to the ringleader."

"If you're right and there's no proof that there's anything damning, then why," Marjorie began looking at the file she had and quoted. "Do they have four armed guards, six lasers, and eight cameras including infrared, guarding that specific vault?" She looked up.

"That's impossible, Marjorie. I am not risking one of my agents on a potential wild goose chase that ends with the hunter getting killed," Kiter stated.

"Sasha killed my wife, nearly killed Nigel and probably called the Rentai Cartel to kill the team. They have weaponized our government against its own civilians. We are all that stands between them and nuclear war. Sasha says the wrong thing to the wrong people, Russia would be up our asses for sure. Not to mention they're buddy-buddy with China. And I doubt seriously on America's help. They have their own issues to sort out right now. They're setting up the chess board to take out the king, literally and figuratively. And I'm not going to let this end up costing British lives. If you don't help me, I'll figure it out on my own."

"It's too risky," Kiter said. "We get caught, even a whiff, and our lives, our families' lives are over with one phone call."

"Then I go alone," Boyd spoke up. All eyes turned to him. "I go in alone. I get caught, disavow me and save yourselves. I have no family left they can hurt. Everyone knows I'm a hothead. I see an impossible situation and I wanna hack it. But, if I don't get caught, we're one step closer to sniffing these bastards out. I get caught or killed? Well, I'll give you a list of hackers to take my place. I'm expendable."

"No, you're not," Rhys said, and Vidar shifted toward Boyd. "No one on this team is expendable. Somm, there's got to be a better way." He looked at his husband. Nigel watched Kiter stare at Boyd. He could practically see the wheels in his head turning.

"You know I'm right, boss," Boyd said.

There was silence for a long time. Gabe held Nigel's hand as they watched the scene unfold. Kiter took a deep breath. "You better not get killed," he finally said, and Boyd relaxed, an easy grin lifting his lips.

"Hey, I'm me. I'm like a cockroach, nothing can kill me," Boyd teased.

"Except a rolled-up newspaper," Vidar grumbled.

"Lovin' the confidence, Thor," Boyd rolled his eyes then leaned over to Marjorie. "Now, Marge, baby, we gotta talk."

To be continued in:

THE CHARING CROSS BOYS

Book Three

I Put a Spell on You

Acknowledgements

Thank you all so much for reading! I loved Gabe Collins and Nigel Sweet since their creation in Kiter's and Rhys' book; Set Fire to the Rain.

The Charing Cross Boys have their origins in *Love Among the Shamrocks Collection, The Next Generation You Don't Own Me* which will be Callum's and Killian's story and was written first but as soon as I wrote the characters of Boyd, Leo, and Callum, I knew they had some sort of story to tell and thus this series began.

If you are interested in some of the external aspects of this book, please take a look at the series or if you would like to meet Vidar in his cameo appearance, please take a look at *Love Among the Shamrocks Universe book one Take My Breath Away.*

I wanted to thank my cousin, Alex, for his military expertise in helping me make the military parts as accurate as I could. Thank you for your service. I love you, brother! Stay safe! I also wanted to thank my beta readers for their contribution and support.

I also have to say thank you to my parents for their love and support during this very difficult time. You mean so much to me and I couldn't imagine going through this tough time without you!

I hope you loved Gabe and Nigel as much as I did! Please consider leaving a review on your favorite site and don't forget to follow me on social media under the handle M. Katherine Clark Author! Be sure to sign up for my newsletter at www.mkatherineclark.net! Keep an eye out for my next release; book three of the series; *The Charing Cross Boys: I Put a Spell on You,* Boyd's and Vidar's story!

Bullying and Homophobia are never okay. If you or a loved one has experienced bullying and would like to speak with someone, please visit stopbullying.gov/resources/get-help-now. If you would like to find ways of helping those who have experienced bullying please visit StopBullying.gov.